ALL ABOUT THE GIRLS
LUX

Kaden Shay

Supposed Crimes LLC • Matthews, North Carolina

Published in the United States.

ISBN: 978-1-938108-93-8

www.supposedcrimes.com

This book is typeset in Goudy Old Style, licensed by Ascender Corporation.

PROLOGUE

Where do I even begin trying to describe my friends? How does one pick a single point which might possibly give even the smallest idea of what these bitches are really like? Don't get me wrong, I adore them all, each and every one of them, but they drive me crazy sometimes. I've known a couple of them for most of my life. The rest kind of filtered in over the years in one way or another and hung around, got attached to the group, and never left.

We're a weird mix and always end up with some very strange looks whenever we're out together, simply because we don't look like we should be friends. I've found the mix leads to some wonderful interactions. I guess maybe the best way to go about this is mostly chronological, so we'll start with my best friend, the girl who has been by my side my entire life.

Angel and I have been best friends since birth, well okay, maybe that's a little bit of a stretch. Her family moved into the house next door to mine when we were four. It was an older neighborhood then, mostly elderly retired couples so we were the only kids in the neighborhood regularly. It made us friends by default. It actually worked out and we clicked and became inseparable by the time school started.

When the other kids in our kindergarten class were being weird and trying to make friends, we had each other. My dad used to say we were connected at the hip, I guess in a way we still are, even though a lot has changed in the years we've been friends. I'll get into that later because it's a long, detailed and slightly sordid story which needs more time than I'm willing to put in right this second.

Angel was always the cute kid, you know the one all the parents loved. The boys pulled her pigtails because they had crushes on her. The girls wished they could be her. This got worse when we hit seventh grade and puberty hit because it hit Angel full on and damn did it do a good job. I mean a really, really good job.

She was always the tallest in the group even before she hit her current five-foot-eleven inches. The height gives her legs most girls would die for. Even at one hundred and sixty-five pounds, not that she would ever admit she is such a weight, her height means she carries it perfectly and I will personally give two hundred dollars to anyone who can find extra fat anywhere on the girls' body. If nothing else, looking for it would be a hell of a lot of fun, but we've looked, believe me, it's not there.

To top it off, she has perfect skin with a perfect tan, perfect waistline, perfect teeth, silky blonde hair almost to her waist, and stunning blue eyes. Okay, okay, maybe I'm a little partial, she is my best friend. It doesn't make those things any less true. Or any less appealing. Unfortunately for the guys out there who are constantly staring at her, she and I came out of the closet at twelve.

That's a whole different story though, and I'll make sure I get into it later on at some point or another, hopefully, maybe, it's possible. Anyway, that's Angel in a nutshell physically, as for her style, well, imagine a typical popular girl in fitted jeans, adorable tops, and expensive shoes and that's Angel. Sometimes I look at her and ask if she's sure she's gay, just to be certain, she always laughs and says she is and to stop being an ass.

Next on the list is Jamie. "James" we call her and she joined our little posse when it was only Angel and I back around the fourth grade. She was a riot even then with her goofball ways and unending antics, a class-clown if there ever was one and always able to make everyone laugh. She's a little spacey sometimes, more ADHD than anything else. It makes hanging out with her hilarious since she's never on one subject for more than a few minutes.

She's the shortest member of the group at only five-foot-two inches but she has a personality big enough for us all. With a joke for almost everything and a one line zinger where she lacks jokes, the group really wouldn't be the same without her. She also happens to be loyal to a fault and one of the best friends a girl could ask for. Always around to pick me up and make me smile when the world knocks me down.

She's the dude of the group and don't even give me a look, she's the first to admit it and she damn well likes it that way. Dark brown hair always in a faux-hawk and forever perfectly styled, typically with a bleach-blonde streak in the front to the left side. The streak and a single piercing in her left eyebrow are her form of rebellion. As well as perpetually dressing like a high school boy. Baggy jeans and either a polo or jersey are her uniform of choice, typically finished off with boots of some kind.

Her deep brown eyes always seem to twinkle with a hint of mischief the rest of us can't seem to keep up with. She's damn cute and she knows it, uses it to her advantage and is almost as bad as I am, almost, but not quite. Occasionally she'll settle down into something like a relationship, but those are rare and typically don't last long, a few weeks, sometimes four or five months.

The next to join our little group, which really isn't very little anymore but it's small enough for us, was Rascal. No, it isn't her real name but she's the youngest of the group, a year younger than the rest of us. Not to mention the fact she's forever in some kind of trouble and can't seem to stay the hell out of it to save her life. Her name is actually Rebecca and she joined the group when we were in sixth grade.

She was the little geek that skipped a grade and ended up in middle school with the rest of us. She's fairly average at five foot five inches with shoulder length brown hair and brown eyes but she's a riot with her pain-in-the-ass ways. Forever in and out of juvie in our early years, the only thing that allowed Rascal to even graduate with the rest of us was the fact she was damn smart and always able to test circles around the rest of us.

Damn genius IQ of hers, it's all at once sexy as hell and irritating as all fuck. We deal with it since she was always willing to help us with homework when we needed it. She's a bit of a tomboy, not nearly as bad as James of course, but rarely seen in anything other than jeans and a tank top. If it's cold she'll add on a hoodie of some kind, but that's about as far as it goes.

She always finishes the look off with a pair of skater shoes. She's best known for her escapades in shoplifting and minor assault, though she stopped getting into as many fights once she hit eighteen and it became a serious offense. The rest of us have always sort of rolled with it since she's never turned those fists of fury on us, so we tend to sit back and watch the show when she puts it on.

Next on the list in the fun parade is Zara. She's like a group of her own within our larger group of friends and doesn't she know it. She joined the group in seventh grade and even then she was absolutely stunning, Jamaican on her fathers' side and Vietnamese on her mothers. She sports a perfect complexion we all hate her for, except Angel, who has skin just as nice, both of them without even trying, the bitches.

Her skin is the color of a smooth caramel mocha and her eyes are so dark they're almost as black as her hair, which, by the way, is perfect too. Yeah, I know, I want to slap her for it half the time. I refrain because even though she's gorgeous at five-foot-seven and a size five, she's the sweetest person anyone could ever meet. She's our good egg, the one that's never been in trouble and always tries to see the good in everyone, even when the rest of us swear there's no good to be had.

She and her girl Dani and the only ones who have been in any kind of decent steady relationship over the past few years. We give them a hard time about it but we love them both and would feel like something was missing if they ever broke up. She's our fashionista and will eagerly tell the majority of us what exactly we are doing wrong in our wardrobes. Rascal, James and I more than the others. She's also our conscience, our sounding board.

Zara is always willing to tell us when we're being ridiculous or talk us down from whatever craziness we're thinking about getting into. She spends a lot of time telling us to calm down and see things from each other's perspective. She's managed to diffuse quite a few spats within the group which, without her, would have been total blowouts and probably ended friendships.

We might as well follow Zara with her girlfriend, Danielle, who graced the group with her presence the same year as Zara, right after we came back to school from Christmas break. The two couldn't be more different, it begins with the physical and goes from there. Where Zara and dark and exotic, Dani is a pale Irish girl, white as can be, almost unruly red hair and green eyes. She has the perfect amount of freckles across her nose and cheeks to make her cute rather than gorgeous.

She's a sweet girl in her own right, at least when dealing with Zara, otherwise she's a bit rough around the edges. She's snarky, sarcastic and has an insult for everything. We love her for it though since she rarely turns it on us and she's normally right on. Zara attempts to keep her from going off the deep end but, hey, she can only keep the girl from her sarcasm for so long.

We think she's damn hilarious but Zara tries to keep her from 'embarrassing us'. If only she knew we're already thinking everything Dani says anyway. She's only half an inch shorter than Zara and roughly the same weight though a little less curvy than her girlfriend. They make a rather odd pair.

They're cute as hell. Which, if I'm being completely honest, makes me want to puke half the time. Anyway, whatever, not talking about my hang-ups here, we're getting to know the group so we'll wrap this one up and move on. Dani is around a lot and we're fine with that, they were both part of the crowd before they started dating and we support them completely, even when we're giving them crap.

We'll move right along to Courtney, or "Court", the only member of the group I haven't fallen into bed with at some point or another. She's our resident virgin, yep, group virgin. Not that I haven't tried valiantly over the last few years. She's waiting until she's married. Yeah, good luck with that girl, let me know when it happens. She's an adorable blonde with slightly longer-than shoulder length hair and hazel eyes. She looks like your typical sorority sister.

She's five-foot-eight, slim built with curves and muscles in all the right places, not that I've looked or anything, well maybe just a little. Whatever. She's a cheerleader, shocking in this group I know, but it's true and she's damn good. She's also a gymnast and a dancer, something we're made painfully aware of whenever we go to the club and she dances circles around us all.

She's actually fairly shy, painfully so most of the time. She only ended up in the group when she transferred to our school in eighth grade and I developed a massive crush on her. She didn't know anyone and so we invited her to sit with us at lunch. By 'we' I mean me of course, who else? She ended up opening up a little around us after a while, even though she refused to return my flirting. I guess she was already onto my game even then.

She grew on us and we adore her. She's our moral compass, not that some of us really listen to the advice she gives us, but we appreciate the thought all the same. At least she cares enough to worry about our eternal souls since most of us couldn't care less about such mundane things. Maybe someday she'll talk James, Rascal, and I into going to church with her, then again, maybe not. Definitely not. I'd hate to have the place burst into flames when I walked through the front door.

I guess that leaves me and my own issues are a path I hate to even start down. I promised though, so here we go anyway. I'm Lux, yes, it really is my name, I swear with everything in me. My parents are a little weird. My father teaches Latin at the local university and my mother teaches Mythology. So here I am, Lux Artemis Marks. I got my mother's practically bleach-blonde hair which I keep fairly short, kind of punk style.

My father gave me his eyes which can't decide if they're blue, green or something between. While they flip between the two colors sometimes, most of the time they just look kind of pale gray which gets me a lot of attention. I am the first to admit I like attention. A lot. I'm a little bit of an attention whore actually, though most of my friends will say flat out whore works best for me. Haters.

I'm five-foot-six inches tall and top in at somewhere around one-hundred and forty pounds. More athletic than anything, I carry myself as such. I'm a tomboy, though not nearly as much so as James. I lean toward skinny jeans, tank tops or muscle shirts and a pair of Converse. I'm a sports nut, though only the playing, not the watching. Give me a ball and I know what to do with it. Well normally, some balls make no sense to me.

I've been out and proud since the summer before eighth grade. By the time we were in high school, I was busy making my way through the female population of Phoenix, Arizona. I'm the first to admit I have a bit of a commitment phobia and the word 'relationship' scares me shitless. I'm not the only one though! That said, I feel like I should walk through a few months in the life of my group of friends.

CHAPTER ONE

Friday, February 13th, 2009 – Mill Avenue, Tempe, Arizona

I found myself standing on the sidewalk out front of yet another bar, or club, or whatever they called this damn place, smoking. I really should try to quit, hear it's really bad for me but, hey, too much effort for the moment and besides, I'm no quitter. I inhaled deeply and closed my eyes, letting the smoke fill my lungs and actually smiling a little. It burned which made the smile wider. Okay I might be a little bit of a masochist but, we all have our issues.

The music in the place behind me was intense, the crowd even more so and I needed a break for a minute. I would head back in soon and rejoin my friends. I had to get a jump on the sad, lonely, just-broke-up-with-my-loser-boyfriend-and-don't-want-to-be-alone-for-Valentine's-Day straight girl crowd before James got her hooks in them. She's almost as good as me, and that's saying something since my track record is pretty damn good.

I pulled in the last of the Camel in my fingers, flicked it into the middle of the street and then turned to head back into the crowded place. I honestly couldn't remember the name of it. It really doesn't matter much anyway, never really cared since we went where the mood led us most nights. I slipped between bodies on the dance floor and made my way to the bar.

Once I managed to order and had my drink in hand, I headed toward the table my friends had taken over. I took in the sight of them standing there and grinned. James was sitting against the wall on the backside of the table so she could scan the room. Zara and

Dani took the real estate to her left. Court and Rascal to her right with Angel standing beside Dani.

I loved my friends and any chance I had to hang out with them was a good night in my book. Even if Zara and Dani were wrapped up in each other all night. Court looked like she would need a month of church when she walked out later. I chuckled as I walked up, giving Rascal a wink when she saw me and holding up a finger to tell her to keep quiet.

She grinned, nodded and winked back. I transferred my drink into my left hand and smacked Angel hard on the ass with my right. She jumped a little then turned and grinned when she saw me but rolled her eyes.

"Aren't you supposed to be picking up a girl tonight?"

"Who says I wasn't doing just that, sexy?"

She hit me with another eye roll and James and I laughed a little. This was the way Angel and I were with each other.

"Mmm, you wish babycakes."

"No need to wish, hit that already, remember? More than once as I recall."

She looked offended for a moment, punched me in the shoulder and then leaned over and kissed my cheek with a little grin.

"You're damn lucky I love you. Bitch."

"I know I am gorgeous. Anyway, who you got your eye on, James?"

A slow grin spread across her face. One of my eyebrows arched up a little. She pointed out onto the dance floor and I followed her finger to the girl she indicated. I laughed and shook my head.

"Yeah, good luck with that buddy. Leave here with that chick before I take someone home and I'll give you fifty bucks tomorrow. But, I win, you owe me fifty."

"You're on, bro."

James got up from the table and headed for the bar. She'd ever been one to approach a lady empty-handed. I had taught her well and she had been a model student. Not to mention she was damn adorable with an easy to fall for charm about her. She gave the bottle the girl had in hand a glance and then ordered two at the bar and made her way onto the dance floor.

"Looks like you're out fifty bucks, babes."

"Oh am I? Guys... Rascal thinks I'm out fifty bucks. What do you think?"

Angel shook her head and Courtney pretended to be very interested in her drink as I grinned at the girl next to me. I accepted her challenge with the smirk and a wink. I leaned over and planted a kiss on my friend, right on the lips. Angel burst out giggling behind me as I left the table and made my way onto the floor.

"Hey, don't glare at me, girl. You asked for it, besides, don't even pretend you don't love it when she kisses you as much as the rest of us do."

I heard the response to what I assumed to be Rascal glaring at her as I walked away. I chuckled to myself. Zara and Dani were about to argue and Court was ten shades of red. I had gotten a decent eye on what was available on my way back in from my smoke break. I knew exactly where I was headed. James had made her life difficult by picking the happy, dancing, fun girl who appeared to be out with her friends. She was hot as hell, sure, but looks weren't everything in this game and she should know it by now.

I wove through the mass of bodies and approached a table in the corner. The girl at the table kept glancing out at a small group of girls on the floor dancing together. She would watch for a few seconds then sigh and stare down at her half-empty drink. She had been nursing the same drink for a while, I had noticed and seemed less than happy to be in the place.

"Hey. You don't look too happy to be here."

I waited until I was close enough I wouldn't have to shout at her but still far enough away to not be all up in her personal space. She looked up at me, confused for a moment and then seemed to realize I was talking to her and just shook her head.

"Lemme guess, friends dragged you out against your will then got all bent outta shape when you didn't wanna dance with them. Am I right?"

She offered me a somewhat sad little smile, glanced out at the group of girls I'd seen her watching all night, and nodded slightly.

"I know the feeling, been there myself. I'm Lux."

I offered her my hand and after thinking about it for a moment she reached over and shook it, progress.

"I'm Leann."

"Nice to meet you, Leann. So tell me, how did you end up here with a group like that and not end up involved in the death of dancing?"

She laughed a little at my mention of her friends terrible dancing and I knew I had her hooked. From what I had seen she hadn't so much as smiled for the last couple hours. Now to reel her in.

"I caught my boyfriend cheating on me a few days ago and they decided I'd been moping around long enough. Guess maybe I had. I just really don't feel up to dancing."

I nodded, having figured it was something along those lines. When she looked up the expression she wore told me a lot. She couldn't believe she had let the words slip out so easily, I was ready for the look, I'd seen it more times than I could count.

"Hey, I'm sorry. That sucks. Men can be real pigs sometimes. I mean, who in their right mind would cheat on you? Look at you."

Even in the dark of the room I saw the blush creep across her cheeks and I knew I was in with this girl.

"Whatever. Thanks for the compliment though, I needed that tonight. Just feels like they dragged me out to cheer me up then forgot about me, ya know?"

"That's a shame. Seems like you could use some one-on-one time right now, not a crowded bar."

She glanced at me and nodded, giving me a look like she couldn't believe I understood her so well. Was it me or was this getting easier the more I did it? I leaned over so I could speak into her ear without shouting, putting me well inside her personal space. As I predicted, she didn't move to pull away.

"Wanna get out of this mad house? Get a coffee or something?"

She tensed beside me for a moment as I slipped my arm around her waist so I leaned back to look at her. I let a slow, easy smile slide onto my face. It was a smile that had melted many women over the years. This one was no different. She thought about it, bit her lower lip and then nodded and reached for her coat.

"I just need to tell my friends I'm leaving."

"Sure thing."

I followed her to the dance floor and over to her friends, and then waited as she told them she was taking off. I couldn't help but grin when I slipped my arm across her shoulders as we headed for the door. I winked at James as we walked past and she glared at me. The leggy blonde she had been after was dancing between her and some guy. She had a lot to learn, but she managed to get hers more often than not and sometimes she even left with someone before me.

I stepped out into the somewhat chilly air. We tugged our coats on then I nodded toward my car. I opened the passenger door for her and she slid into the seat, getting settled as I walked around and hopped into the drivers' seat.

"So, where to?"

She sat there and thought for a minute, her eyes on her hands and I took the time to remind her why she had said she'd leave with me. I leaned over a little and put my hand over hers where they were clasped in her lap and kissed her neck lightly. I heard the sharp little intake of breath. The little shudder flashing through her vibrated across my hand and I smiled. She was so done and she didn't even know it yet. Or maybe she did and didn't care. Either way, this deal was sealed.

"Southern and Gilbert, I'll give you directions from there."

I nodded, squeezed her hands and dropped another light kiss on her neck before I started up the car. I smiled to myself as I followed her directions, ending where I figured we would. Needless to say we weren't at a coffee house but instead in front of a small house off Gilbert behind the high school. I parked and we made our way to the front door, stopping on the porch before she unlocked the door.

"Um, I have roommates and at least one is probably home so, try and keep it down."

I nodded my agreement and grinned as I wondered how long she'd be following her own 'keep it down' rule once I got started on her. We stepped inside and I followed her to the kitchen, leaning against the counter while she made coffee. It was cute that she was bothering when we both knew coffee wasn't why she'd brought me here. We could have gone anywhere for the drink.

"I've, uh, never done this before."

I let out a soft laugh and accepted a mug from her. I set it on the counter and took her hand in mine. I tugged her until she was pressed against me and kissed her before she could argue. She started to protest and to pull away but then decided against it and pressed in closer, deepening the kiss. My left hand tangled in her dirty-blonde hair and my right slid down to her hip, and then around her waist, pulling her closer as her arms wrapped around my shoulders. I let the kiss go on until I felt her starting to lean against me for support. Then I leaned back and gave her a second to catch her breath.

"Bedroom?"

She nodded and pulled away, leading me back to her bedroom and closing the door. I didn't bother taking in the room, I really didn't care. I only had one thing on my mind and, so did she. I pulled her shirt over her head and dropped it on the floor as I backed her toward the bed. She fought getting my shirt off. As cute as the struggle was, I finally helped her out then tossed my tank top by the door. It would make it easier to find later on.

We'd reached the point of being a little more than halfway across the room. I was done playing so I pulled her back in and kissed her, hard. My hands slid down under her ass and I pulled her up into my arms. Her legs went around my waist as I crawled into the middle of her double bed. I pinned her under me, never losing her lips. I reached around and made quick work of the hooks on her bra with my thumb and middle finger. After yanking the thing off I threw it, not caring where it landed and then helped her get mine off. It got tossed near my shirt by the door.

I broke the kiss to trail my lips down her jawline, neck and chest, pausing to run my tongue over her left nipple. The sound of her gasp spurred me on. I pulled it into my mouth and sucked on it, eliciting a soft moan from her. I decided to push it some so I bit down and she whimpered. A smile crossed my face at the sounds I was bringing out of this one. I continued working her left nipple as I let my right hand slip down over her bare stomach. I tickled around her belly button making her squirm under me. I popped the button on her jeans, working the zipper down one handed and eased my hand inside the tight denim.

She wasn't wearing any panties, dirty girl, and made my job easier, or at least faster. I trailed my fingers down between her legs. She was wet as hell already but I teased her anyway making her writhe under my hand. I'm pretty sure I heard her beg me to stop the teasing. How about that? Never one to let a girl down I only made her beg for a minute before I moved my mouth to her right nipple.

As my mouth moved I dipped two fingers inside her but only to the second knuckle. The moan she let out was punctuated by her fingers wrapping into my short hair and tugging on it. It was going to be like that was it? I twisted my head to pull my hair from her grip so I could move better. Once I was free I pulled my left hand from under her body and used it to work her jeans off her hips. Clothing could really get in the way.

I kicked her shoes off, following them with her jeans and ran my tongue down her stomach as I lowered myself down her body. She had picked up begging again and, I won't even lie, it was sexy as hell. I wanted to hear more of it so I stopped right as my lips hovered between her legs. She whined, actually whined at me. I remove my fingers from her to blow a light stream of cold air over her heated core.

She gasped, whimpered and squirmed under me. The begging started again as I reached my left hand up and spread it against her stomach. Her movement had gotten annoying so I held her to the bed. I leaned in close and my fingers slid into her as my tongue flicked out against her clit, drawing a moan out of her. She tried to stifle the sound with her arm and got close to succeeding.

My fingers easily picked up a rhythm. It was matched by her hips as she thrust down against my upstroke. This girl knew exactly what she was doing despite her claims she'd never done this before. I simply let my tongue match the rhythm against her clit. I curled my fingers up slightly with each stroke. The action hit its target and made her back arch up off the bed as her moans grow louder. I pulled her clit between my lips and sucked it, biting down gently before returning to flicking it with my tongue.

With each round she got louder. Muscles tightened, gripping my fingers tightly and I knew she was almost at her peak. I pushed her over the edge. A scream ripped from her as she came. So much for being quiet, then again, they rarely were once I got my hands on them. Her muscles twitched and flexed around my fingers for a few seconds before she came down off her climax. I wasn't about to allow it to end so quickly. I let her slip partway into the delirium of afterglow then started pushing her buttons again. My movements worked at edging her back to the peak.

The second orgasm didn't take nearly as long as the first and was a lot stronger. She reacted by reaching one hand up to grab her headboard as the nails of the other dug sharply into my shoulder. Battle scars, I loved it, proof I had given her a night she wouldn't soon forget. Savoring the sting of the scratches, I relented and let her come down. I waited until she had relaxed then removed my fingers, wiping my hand on her blanket as she pulled me up to kiss me again.

She returned the favor and I had to admit she wasn't half bad. I was thankful for it since screamers always turned me on. I was in desperate need of a climax. Once she passed out I slipped out of the bed, tugged on my clothes and eased her door open silently. I eased it closed without a sound then headed back down the hall to let myself out. I didn't quite make it and was instead met with her roommates. The three women looked at me like they weren't sure what to make of me. Or maybe they couldn't makes sense of what they had heard coming from their roommates' bedroom.

"Hey, you're that chick from the bar."

I raised an eyebrow as I recognized one of the friends and nodded.

"Getting coffee my ass. Oh well, at least she stopped moping."

I adopted my usual cocky post-conquest grin as they laughed, and then I made my exit. I couldn't remember ever being in the mood to get to know roommates. I had been ready to go home and get some sleep the second she drifted off.

Outside, I hopped into my car and headed toward the house I shared with Angel, James and Rascal. We lived out in the middle of nowhere people called San Tan Valley. The peace and quiet was worth the drive.

After a drive during which I slapped myself several times to stay awake I pulled into our driveway. I locked my car and made my way into the house to find my three roommates sitting in the living room. The TV played a lesbian movie but they didn't seem to be watching it.

"Well hey there playa."

I smirked at Angel's comment as I tugged Rascal up out of my favorite chair. She had developed a habit of sitting in it, knowing what would happen. I figured the move gave me a free pass for my reaction so I continued it despite other seats being available. I flopped into the big plush monster, pulled her back into my lap and let my arms fall around her waist. She snuggled right in, perfectly content sitting on me and I gave her hip a light squeeze.

"So, how was she?"

So like Rascal, right to the point like always which made me beam.

"Fine. Screamer."

"Oh we know how much you like those. You get yours too or need some friendly help?"

I let out a laugh at her then ruffled her hair as I shook my head.

"Well, she managed to give me something before she passed out. But you know Ras, if you want in my bed again, just say so."

I winked at her and she rolled her eyes at me, ending it on a rough nudge with her shoulder.

"Whatever."

"And by 'whatever' she means that of course she does."

I snorted as Rascal threw a bottle cap at James, and then leaned in and nuzzled her neck.

"Stop that."

She swatted at me playfully and I grinned at her. I knew either one of us could say the word and the other would be undressed in a second. Rascal and I had shared a special kind of friendship since the tenth grade and it had always seemed natural to us. She wasn't the player James and I were, she didn't have it in her. So when she wasn't dating, she would come to me to help ease the tension when it got to be too much.

Never one to complain I went right along with it. She was cute as hell and damn good in bed so it was a win-win. It had always amazed me girls left her so quickly. Best I could figure was they weren't smart enough to keep up with her and she started getting bored with them.

"Why would I do that?"

"Didn't you say you just got laid?"

"And? Like anyone holds up to you in that department, come on Ras."

I ran my tongue up the edge of her ear. She shivered against me and smacked my arm.

"Damn you. Fine, but you're showering and brushing your damn teeth first. I draw the line at tasting some other ho on you."

I bit back my laugh at the comment as she slid off my lap. I got out of the chair after her. We waved goodnight to Angel and James and they both grinned and shook their heads at us.

"Why don't you just shower with me, then you can be sure I'm clean."

I purred the words into her ear as I pulled her back against my chest on our way down the short hallway off the living room to my bathroom. I had the only bedroom and bathroom downstairs in the four bedroom, four bath house. I was the most likely to stumble in at all hours half asleep or falling down drunk so I was voted into it. We had barely gotten the bathroom door closed before clothes started coming off and the shower was started. Rascal loved shower sex and I was more than willing to oblige the sexy little brunette whenever I could. No one would catch me complaining but I refused to examine the situation too closely.

CHAPTER TWO

Saturday, February 14th, 2009 – San Tan Valley, Arizona

I woke up Saturday morning and had a moment of panic when I felt my arm across another body. There was a flash of terror as my mind thought I had let myself fall asleep at some girls' house. I hated having to deal with the awkward morning after bullshit so I avoided it at all costs. I took a deep, shaky breath and the scent that hit me calmed me instantly. I would know the combination of coconut and brown sugar anywhere. I allowed myself to relax as I tightened my arm and pulled Rascal closer.

I once again avoided examining why I let things happen with her and no one else. The reality of what it might mean frightened me. Instead of thinking I buried my face into the back of her neck, a small happy noise slipping from me. We were both completely naked, her back pressed against my chest. I had my arm around her waist and our legs were tangled together.

There was a pounding on my door, the sound made me grumble and make a face into the back of Rascals' neck. About two seconds passed before James threw my bedroom door open.

"Hey, wake up jackass. If we're late for work Mr. Kane is gonna kill us. Or fire us."

I growled at the mention of my boss, hating the man more every day James worked for him. The hatred reached a new level today since we were being forced to work Saturdays for the next month.

"Jesus... Angel!"

She shouted for our fourth roommate as she retreated from my room, a sure sign I was about to be told on.

"What?"

"Can you please go unwind your best friend from around Rascal and make her get dressed?"

"Sure thing. Go finish breakfast. Lux. Come on, seriously. Get up."

Angel picked up a throw pillow off the couch, walked down the hall and lobbed it at my head. It hit Rascal and me both, earning a grumble from me and a yelp from my bedmate before she threw it back.

"Not cool, morning bitch."

Angel laughed at Rascal as I rolled over, sticking her tongue out at us. Neither of us gave a damn about the fact we were completely nude. Our friends had seen it all by this point in our lives.

"Whatever, we're getting up okay? Go away."

Angel nodded and removed herself from my doorway. She left the door open since we would be up and moving in a couple minutes. Once Rascal was awake we were golden, she was the tough one to wake up.

"Morning."

She grinned down at me before she leaned in and planted a kiss on my lips. I smiled back, returned the kiss and then stretched.

"Morning gorgeous. Better get moving before James murders me."

"Yeah, that would suck. Come on."

We crawled out of my bed and she collected her clothes from my bathroom with a yawn. I got one last kiss before she made her way up to her bedroom. I shuffled to my closet and rummaged around in it for something decent to wear to work. Eventually I tugged on a pair of black slacks and a baby blue button down shirt. I rolled the sleeves up right below my elbows, tucked it in and slipped a black belt through the loops. I stared at the closet trying to remember what I needed next then snapped my fingers as it hit me.

I dug out a clean pair of black socks and pulled on my work boots, freshly shined after work the day before. I yawned again, still worn out in the best way, and then made my way toward the bathroom. The rest of my morning ritual included brushing my teeth and taming my hair. The hair was always a feat after a night with Rascal. I laughed and with my hair mostly tamed, headed into the kitchen. I intentionally bumped James with my hip and grinned at her when she turned on me.

"You owe me fifty bucks, shithead."

She grumbled as she threw some money at me then took her coffee and a bagel to the dining table. I couldn't help it, I chuckled at her as I scooped the money off the floor. I quickly doctored a mug of coffee and dropped some eggs and bacon onto a plate.

I hated working on Saturdays, but when the boss put his foot down we all jumped to do as he said. If we didn't we risked his wrath, not something we enjoyed. James and I worked as networking techs and apparently the university was having some computer lab issues. This was best accomplished while students weren't attempting to use the lab for classes.

We finished our breakfast then headed out for work. The work day was slow and boring. Saturdays sucked when we were forced to work rather than be out with our friends. We would make up for it that night when we hit the club together. It would mean a second chance at conquest for poor James. I was in a good mood as I finished my work for the day.

I waved goodbye to James then headed out to my car. I had been ready for a night out since I'd climbed out of bed. James would be at least another hour, working more slowly and diligently than I normally did. My work wasn't bad or sub-par, I simply managed it faster. I put my car in park as Angel pulled in beside me and I waved at her. We both exited our vehicles and headed toward the front door together.

"How was work?"

"About as good as work can really be on a Saturday."

"I hear ya. What's the plan for tonight?"

"No clue yet, girlie, I need to call everyone and see what's up. Court will probably only hang out for a couple hours. You know all about her need to be at church on Sunday mornings."

I chuckled and Angel nodded in agreement. It was something we could always count on for Saturday nights ~ Court leaving by midnight. She needed to get plenty of sleep before Sunday morning services.

"Why don't you call Court and I'll give Zara a ring... Where's Ras?"

"Sure thing. Rascal met someone at lunch today, they kinda hit it off and she might not go out with us tonight."

The information hit me in the gut and brought me up short as I processed it but I shook it off as quickly as I could.

"Oh, all right."

I tried to sound casual, like nothing had happened when she'd dropped that bomb on me. Angel knew me better than that though and she tossed a knowing look in my direction. It made me want to squirm. I hated that she could read me so well.

"What was that, Angel?"

"What was what?"

"That look."

"You know exactly what the look is about. Little upset Rascal won't be out with us tonight? Little jealous she met someone?"

"Pfft, whatever. I just know how fast she can get attached to new people and I hate having to watch her fall apart when they leave."

I got the look again and I rolled my eyes and turned away from her. I didn't want to deal with her analyzing of my reactions.

"If you say so. I'll go call Court, back in a bit."

She left the room, giving me the privacy I needed for the moment and I took a much needed deep breath. I pulled my cell phone out of my pocket and flipped through my contacts to Zara. I tapped the call button, popping in my Bluetooth while it rang and waiting for her to pick up.

"Hey Lux, sup?"

"Hey brat, you and Dani coming out with us tonight?"

"Of course! Just text me so I know where we're meeting and we'll be there!"

"Awesome, see ya later."

"Bye."

I hung up with Zara and stared at my phone as I scrolled through my contacts, biting my lower lip. I tried to decide if I should make the call my brain was considering. I finally gave in and tapped the call button beside the name. I pulled in a deep breath and waited for an answer. It never came but the message clicked on causing the same grin as always as it played through my Bluetooth.

'You just missed Rascal bitches. Leave a message and if I don't hate you, I'll hit you back. Later!'

I rolled my eyes, shaking my head at her outgoing message for at least the hundredth time. Against my better judgement I decided to leave a message for her. The choice came right as it beeped telling me to start speaking.

"Hey Ras, it's Lux. Just checking in to see if you wanted to go out with us tonight. Text me if you're in. Later gator."

I ended the call glad I had sounded mostly normal then tossed my Bluetooth on the counter. Angel cleared her throat behind me, making me jump. I turned around to face her. She had one of her eyebrows raised at me and a small, satisfied smirk appeared on her face.

"What now?"

"Just couldn't resist could you?"

"Dunno what you're talking about."

"Mmhmm, okay girl, I'll let you have your delusion. So Zara and Dani coming?"

I was glad for the change of subject and nodded in response. I decided it wasn't too early to start getting ready and vacated the kitchen, hoping to leave the weird feelings behind as well. I ducked into my room to pick out my clothes. Outfit sorted, I locked myself in the bathroom and took my time getting cleaned up. I could admit I was hiding, not interested in having Angel pick me apart any further.

Once I was clean, I took my sweet time getting dressed and making myself presentable, and then popped into my bedroom. Even though I knew it made me a sad excuse of a human being, I decided to check my phone. I needed to see if I had heard from Rascal. No such luck and I didn't give myself a chance to overthink why it bothered me. Instead I pulled on my shoes and headed out into the living room.

I'd heard James come home while I was in the shower. Zara and Dani had shown up while I was getting dressed. Even knowing more of my group of friends was in the house, I took my time walking down the very short hallway. I stepped out and grinned at the small group gathered on the furniture as they turned to wave at me. Even the smiles on their faces didn't completely fix my mood.

"Hey guys. Everyone ready to go?"

A chorus of 'yes' went up from the group and we grabbed keys and coats and headed out. There was a few minutes of standing in the driveway chatting. We were trying to decide who would be the designated driver for the night. It came down to myself or James and we played a short, three round set of rock-paper-scissors to decide. I lost. Damn. I've always hated being the designated driver. I prefer to have a few drinks in me before I play my games. Not to mention making it hard to run home with someone when I had a bunch of drunks to chauffeur around.

Fuck, fuck, fuck. This was so not what I needed. I needed to be shit-faced and not thinking about a certain adorable brunette. I fought to keep my mind from wandering too far as I drove Dani's

Suburban. I really didn't want to wreck the thing and risk her wrath. We decided on a place and I pointed the loaded vehicle in the right direction. The chatter in the backseats drifted over me, keeping my train of thought off my turmoil while I drove.

I pulled in and focused on parking once we arrived then everyone piled out of the vehicle. I needed a cigarette before we went inside.

"Go grab a table guys. I'll catch up in a few."

James and Angel shot each other a look, Angel rolled her eyes, James shrugged and then they headed inside to save a table. I spent three or four minutes staring at traffic going by on the street. The pack of Camels rested forgotten in my hands, twirling between my fingers. I finally pulled one out, brought it to my lips then started checking my pockets for my constantly missing lighter. After patting a few spots I finally located it in the small pocket on the right side of my jeans. I dug it out and flicked it a few times until it stayed lit.

I held it to the tip of the cigarette, inhaled until it glowed red and then put the lighter in the pack this time. I tucked the pack back into my pocket for later. I leaned back against the SUV, my right foot propped against the front driver's side tire. My cigarette held in my right hand, left hand in my pocket I had a mental flash of a James Dean photo and managed a small smile. I let my vision blur for the time it took me to smoke the cigarette, staring out into the street. I finished the first Camel and took a deep breath of fresh air.

After a few beats I decided, why the hell not and fished another out of the pack. I lit it and shoved everything back where it had been. I took my time smoking the second cigarette and flicked the butt into the parking lot. I checked my watch and decided I had a few seconds to be sad again then checked my phone. No messages, no missed calls. Awesome. I huffed and pushed away from the vehicle behind me to head into the building.

I stepped into the building, having to give my eyes a minute to adjust to the flickering of the lights inside. I scanned the tables for my group. Despite the pain tightening my heart, I couldn't stop the grin that spread across my face when I spotted them. They were already holding drinks, an extra sitting on the table in front of an open seat. Looked like someone had ordered my usual designated driver night water with lime.

I let out a soft chuckle as I made my way toward them. Upon arrival I gave Angel's hair a little tug and smacked Courtney on her cute little ass. It made her yelp and turn at least five shades of red. It made everyone burst into a round of laughter. Well, everyone except Court who seemed to be contemplating hiding under the table. It was so damn easy to push her buttons, sometimes it almost wasn't fun, but only almost. It managed to entertain me most of the time so I kept doing it. The tomato-colored Court shrank into herself slightly and I felt bad for a minute. It made me reach over and wrap an arm around her shoulders.

"You know I'm just raggin' on ya. Right?"

She offered me a barely perceptible nod and a tiny smile. Thankfully the blush stayed in place on her cheeks. Sometimes it made her look fourteen years old again.

"Good... So, now, James, my good friend, what do we have our eye on tonight?"

I finally picked up my glass and took a drink as I looked across the table at James. The right side of her lips quirked into a sly smirk in my direction. I raised an eyebrow, wondering what on earth she had up her sleeve. I hoped she had better taste than the night before since she'd obviously left alone. I caught myself shifting to scan the room through my peripheral vision to take in what James had to choose from.

A decent crowd was in the place and there were numerous lovely ladies present. She could go either way with the night. She might get lucky. I glanced back across the table and she shot a quick glance toward the wall just opposite us. I followed the flicker of direction and smirked when I saw who she had her eye on. Much better choice than the night before and right up her alley in so many ways.

"Go for it girl," I said.

She nodded as she slid from her seat. She started across the room. I decided to make my way around the table and then took her seat against the wall to watch her work her magic. I leaned it back so it was balanced on the two back legs. The upper back rail met the wall lightly, keeping the thing propped up. I gave the crowd another once over as Angel eyed me purposefully. She raised one eyebrow in my direction, her head tilted slightly to the left.

"What?"

"You gonna get your ass out there and play a little?"

"Nah."

"Seriously?"

"Yeah. Not tonight."

"Why?"

The last question came from Court, throwing me somewhat. I looked between the two of them and then glanced at Zara and Dani. They were looking at me like I had grown two heads.

"What do you mean?"

I returned my gaze to Courtney as I replied, dismissing the looks the other three were shooting my general direction.

"You know exactly what I mean Lux. This is what you do, we go out Friday and Saturday nights, you pick up some poor, unsuspecting and more-than-likely straight girl, take her home, presumably rock her world and then leave before she wakes up. Sound about right?"

There was a tight undercurrent to her voice. It was a bite I wasn't used to hearing from any of my friends, least of all Courtney.

"Court... It's not really like..."

"Sure it's not. Of course, because, as far as you're concerned, as long as they get off, you've done your job and they must be happy so it doesn't matter if they wake up alone, confused and even a little crushed because that isn't your problem, is it? No, it's not since you don't give a damn about anyone but yourself and your own feelings."

I gaped at her after she cut me off mid-sentence. I had no idea where the hostility came from. I didn't get the chance to ask her what her issue was. The moment I attempted to open my mouth she rolled her eyes and slammed her glass down on the table. With a shove her chair moved back and she high-tailed it from the room.

I sat in stunned silence, staring at the space my friend had occupied. My mind tried to process what the hell had happened. I had no clue what the outburst had been about. I could admit I had expected something like it eventually though not from Courtney. Angel, Zara or Dani sure, maybe even James but not her. I'd never talked her into going to bed with me, never done to her the things I had done to the others. I couldn't understand what I might have done to make her so hostile.

I finally recovered and looked around the table. The looks I got from the other three told me they might be as stumped as me. It was crazy but I knew I needed to give Court a chance to cool off and then I would make an attempt to talk to her.

"Do any of you know what the hell that was all about?"

I glanced around the table as they all shook their heads then exhaled loudly and ran my hand through my hair. I finished what was left of the water in my glass and stared into the ice I had left. My mind grasped at strings.

"Hey. I just saw Court take off. She looked kinda miffed. Everything okay over here?"

I looked up when I heard the familiar tone of James' voice and shook my head in confusion as I responded.

"Wish we knew dude."

"Yeah, she just blew the hell up at Lux and then stormed out."

The confusion in Zara's voice was apparent, matching my expression and James raised an eyebrow.

"Seriously? What did she blow up about? I mean, what did she say?"

Zara, Dani and Angel began replaying the speech including the moments which had happened right before and after. I tuned them out, not really wanting to hear it again. Once was one time too many for the night. I glanced up when things went silent at the table and saw James standing there. Her eyes had gone wide and she looked as stunned as the rest of us.

I wanted to know why Courtney was so irate with me which meant I had no choice about the eventual impending conversation. At least since no one knew anything more than I did. I let out a ragged sigh and shook my head as James shrugged then moved toward the bar. I kept an eye on her as she grabbed two drinks and made her way back to the girl she'd been hitting on.

I used the thumb and middle finger of my right hand to rub my temples, trying to staunch the oncoming headache. I spent the rest of the night zoned out attempting to figure out what was happening with my normally shy friend. This inattention caused me to jump when I felt a hand on my shoulder. I looked over to find Angel standing on my left looking down at me.

"Hey, we're ready to head home. You want to get out of here?"

I nodded and slid from my chair. There was a second glass of water with lime someone had ordered for me at some earlier point sitting full on the table. I stuffed my hands in my pockets and shuffled toward the door with my friends. It wasn't until we reached the SUV that I realized James was nowhere to be found. I guessed she had managed to leave with the girl she'd been flirting with. Even that couldn't distract me enough for a smile. It had been a disappointing night at every turn. We climbed into the vehicle but sat there unmoving for five minutes. I had to pull my concentration together enough to actually perform as the designated driver I promised to be.

We unloaded at the house. Zara and Dani would either spend the night on our futon or one would drink enough coffee to get them safely home. I hadn't paid any attention to how much either of them had downed at the bar. When Angel vanished into her bedroom and then returned with some extra sweats and tees I figured they were staying. I was fine with it, they normally stayed a few nights a month. We had come to expect it when they drank too much. I left the three of them to chat after Zara and Dani changed and wandered back toward the front of the house.

I stopped on my way to sprinkle some food into our sixty gallon fish tank. I stood there watching the collection of cichlids fight over the food, distracted. I tried to convince myself I wasn't doing exactly what I knew I was doing ~ Practicing time wasting and avoidance. I looked at the bookshelves for a minute as if scanning it for a book to read then gave up. I went through the laundry room and pulled open the door leading into the garage. It was empty, though I had expected as much and I let the door close again. I attempted to ignore the heaviness settled in the pit of my stomach, finding it hard to do so.

I moved back through the house, hands in my pockets, eyes on my shoes. I made a point of not looking at my three friends as I headed toward my room. I shut the door, locked it and sat down on my bed, eyes still down. My elbows rested on my knees, hands hanging limply in front of them. I glanced over at my clock and was shocked to find it was barely one in the morning. We had to have left the bar right after midnight to have made it home so early. I stayed there, sitting on the edge of my bed and staring blankly at the wall for a while. I was content letting time slip by and not really paying attention to it, or anything else.

I finally stood up, kicked off my shoes and flipped the light off. I sprawled out on my bed, fully clothed and let my eyes close. A last glimpse at the clock had told me it was about to be four in the morning. It took some fighting with mind and heart but I finally drifted off into a fitful and restless sleep.

I woke with a start to someone banging on my door. I peeked one eye open toward the blinds to confirm the sun was at least up then glanced at my clock. It was only minutes after eight and I had barely been asleep for four hours. It wasn't nearly enough sleep to manage a good mood, even a faked one. The banging came again and I growled at the offending noise which was giving me a headache. I was far too early in the morning for anyone to be waking me.

I heaved myself into a sitting position on my tangled blankets and sheets. I must have tossed and turned a lot throughout the night to have destroyed my bed coverings so thoroughly. I leaned over, flipped the lock on my doorknob and pulled it open. I got a look at James through the one eye that was open.

"What?"

"Get up."

"No. Go away."

"Lux, seriously, stop being all gruff and get your ass out of bed."

"Why? Why do I need to get up right now? Seriously James, I didn't get to sleep until after four and I'm exhausted."

"Should have known you'd pick someone up last night. Angel said you didn't, you just brought them home but they fell asleep around one thirty. I told her you probably went back out and met someone. You dog."

I didn't bother correcting her assumptions, not wanting to get into what had actually kept me up. She grinned as she reached over and gave me a little shove on the front of my shoulder. Had I been standing it might have actually toppled me.

"Well, whatever, that's your own damn fault. Right now, I just got off the phone with Cara, she wants me to come over for the day and bring you and Angel."

Cara was James' rather adorable cousin. I hadn't bothered to tell my friend I had hooked up with her relative in our sophomore year of college. She wasn't gay, at least, not once we finished school. She was one of those girls, the 'gay until graduation' crowd. Given the information, I hadn't seen the need to complicate our friendship with the hookup. I chuckled and nodded to let her know I was agreeing to the ordeal then pushed up off my bed to get ready.

It took me thirty minutes to be showered, dressed, have my hair styled and be out in the living room waiting with James. Being who she was, it always took Angel at least twice as long as the two of us to get ready. We were used to it after so many years though and we had learn patience. She finally joined us and we headed out and piled into James' car. I let Angel have shotgun, needing some time in my own head and knowing the drive would be perfect. As I expected, she and James fell into a conversation punctuated by top forty hits coming through the speakers around us. Thoughts spun around in my brain and while nothing settled in for long I did spend quite a bit of it wondering what was going on with Court.

By the time we pulled up to Cara's house I had decided I needed to let it go until I could actually talk to her. We exited the car and made our way up to the front door, James and Angel joking and poking each other the whole way. They had always behaved like sisters and normally watching them would make me laugh. Today I didn't have it in me. I was a prisoner to my own mind and it sucked. I heaved out a sigh and hurried to catch up to my friends as James rang the doorbell. It took some work to get my expression under control and I hoped I pulled it off. I was right behind them with what I prayed was an acceptably believable fake smile on my face when Cara opened the door.

She welcomed us then led us through to the rest of the crowd in the backyard. Somehow I managed to make it through five hours at her house without anyone realizing I didn't want to be there. We finally caught a break when James said we needed head out. Apparently we had things to finish before the work week started again the next day. I couldn't remember the things she might be talking about but I wasn't about to argue. I wanted to get away from everyone, go home and lock myself in my room again.

We slipped back into our seats in the car and headed back toward home. The conversation started up in the front seat again as I drifted back into my head. I was so distracted Angel had to open the door and shake me to get my attention when we pulled into the driveway. The action snapped me back to the moment. I gave her a slightly embarrassed smile before exiting the car and going about my usual Sunday night routine on auto-pilot.

CHAPTER THREE

Friday, February 20th, 2009 – Mesa, Arizona

The week had been a total blur. I had worked a lot and tried to be social so my friends wouldn't worry too much. So far they had only seemed to give me the most subtle and fleeting of worried or confused glances. If they held more than passing worry, they hadn't said anything. I was thankful for it and hoped I could keep it up through the night since we were, once again, out for a night on the town. It was fairly normal for one of our weekends but I wasn't feeling it for more than one reason.

The first was Court refusing to speak to me all week. Whatever I had done had left her really pissed at me for reasons I didn't understand. It was starting to depress me on top of being confusing. I wasn't used to having one of my friends so angry with me, definitely not her. She was always the sweet one, the one who was there when someone else treated one of us in such an awful way. That made it worrying and confusing me all at once. To add a little insult to that specific injury, my secondary reason was not having seen Rascal all week.

She'd come home, sure, Angel and James had seen her so I knew she'd been in the house. However she had been either in and out while I was at work or already asleep by the time I got in. I kept missing her which was making me feel awkward and out of sorts. I didn't want to examine it too closely. I was scared of what it might mean, so I let it go and refused to think about it much. Somehow not thinking about her, or the situation, was harder when she wasn't around. I decided it was because I didn't have her there distracting me from thinking about it. I was in a funk and it was definitely showing.

I sat at the table my friends had claimed in the corner and stared at my glass. James had taken a spot looking over my shoulder, out into the room from against the wall across the table. Zara and Dani were attached at the lips as usual. I didn't even have it in me to hassle them about it, which was pathetic. Angel was chatting excitedly with James about something as she continued to scan the room. She was on the hunt again. I would normally give the crowd a glance and try to guess what she'd go for but I didn't really care tonight. Angel had been named designated driver and I should have been a couple drinks in and taking in the crowd with James.

At the moment all I wanted to do was go home and crawl into bed. Being alone to stare at nothing and fall asleep sounded perfect, yet very depressing.

"Hey, you okay girl? You seem kinda off."

Angel's voice jarred me out of the almost pleasant thought of my pillows. I turned my gaze up toward her, taking a few seconds to process her words.

"Huh? Oh, um, yeah, I'm okay. Think I may be coming down with something. Long work hours this week and they wore me out. You know how not sleeping makes me sick."

The excuse sounded legitimate to me and even though her eyes told me she didn't buy it she nodded. I was thankful she was allowing me to hold tight to my denial. I figured it would come crashing down around my feet eventually. I wouldn't let eventually be tonight. I finally talked myself into drinking what was in my glass and then told the girls I needed to step outside. They probably figured I needed a cigarette and let me go without much noise.

I crossed the room, barely paying attention to the people present. A slightly-chilled breeze hit me when I stepped outside and I let it wash over me. It didn't do much to stifle the fiery swirl of confusion, hurt and anger roiling inside me. I considered having a cigarette, and then changed my mind, left the pack in its place in my pocket and started down the street. I wasn't sure where I was headed. Home was at least an hour drive away. Since it was already nine-thirty at night, I wouldn't be walking home.

I sighed into the chilled desert air. My warm breath left a thin white cloud hanging in front of me for several seconds before dissipating. I pulled my jacket tighter around me and exhaled a huff.

Might be hotter than the seventh circle of hell here in the summer midday, but after dark in February it could be brutal and damn near freezing. I shivered slightly despite my jacket but kept walking. I couldn't find it in me to care where I ended up. I just wanted to keep moving.

A few people bumped into me as they entered and exited the busy clubs and bars. I kept my head down, eyes on my shoes, hands shoved deep into the pockets of my jacket and walked. I lost track of time as I soldiered on. After a while the cigarette I considered earlier sounded good after all. When I stopped to pull one out and looked up I shook my head at where I had ended up. Somehow I had managed to wander to the corner of Priest and University. All I had to do was walk a couple blocks and I would be at Courtney's place.

It took me about ten seconds to decide I had landed on that specific corner for a reason. I made the turn and kept walking, forgetting the cigarette. I paused at the corner of the street I needed, able to see Court's house three down the block. I sighed before urging myself forward. I'd come this far, no reason to stop, not when I needed answers. I walked up to the house, onto the porch and rang the doorbell, and then waited to see if anyone would answer. There were lights on inside so I figured someone was up and ringing the bell would be okay.

Footfalls let me know someone was approaching. I steadied myself as the door swung open. I'd only ever been to her house three times and had never been inside. Actually, I couldn't remember even making it up to the door. She had always met us on the sidewalk when we picked her up for things. I considered the thought for only a second before taking in the sight that greeted me when the door opened. It stunned me to the point I couldn't help but stare in shock at the man who had answered.

He was big, at least six-foot-three by my estimation and well over two-hundred and fifty pounds. He sported close cropped, dark brown hair graying slightly at the temples. The same dazzling hazel eyes Courtney had blazed at me from a very stern expression. I placed him in his fifties somewhere and decided this must be her father, weird since I didn't think any of us had ever met the man.

"Can I help you?"

"Uh, yeah, I'm... Uh, here to see Courtney. Is she home?"

He seemed to consider me for a moment, giving me a once over as if trying to figure out why I would be asking for her.

"Just a minute."

He finally replied before he moved away, shutting the door to a crack as he walked back into the house. I heard another set of lighter footfalls and figured it must be Courtney coming to the door.

"What do you want?"

Her sharp tone slapped me right in the face, the words only making it sting more. She stood there, anger written on her face, arms crossed over her chest. I knew she didn't want to talk to me, but I had to try.

"Court, can we talk?"

"Why?"

"Because I need to talk to you about last week."

"That's tough, Lux because I really don't want to talk to you. Not right now, maybe not for a while."

A heavy weight crushed down on my insides, making the knot forming in the pit of my stomach impossible to ignore. I didn't know what to do to fix whatever had made her so angry with me. I didn't even know what I'd done but I had to try, having one of my friends so angry at me hurt..

"Please, just give me a few minutes."

She seemed to consider the request and for a split second I thought she was going to tell me to get lost. Instead she sighed and grabbed her jacket from the nearby rack. She shut the door behind her as she slipped into the jacket and then nodded to the swing on the porch across the street.

"No one lives there right now, we can sit there for a few."

I nodded and followed her lead across the street then settled onto the swing with her on my right. I gripped the edge of the swing harder than needed and my fingers start to numb from the pressure.

"You wanted to talk, so talk."

I took a deep breath and looked over at her as I tried to decide what to do. If I out and asked what I'd done she'd only get irritated about the fact I didn't know since I obviously should.

"Look, obviously my behavior has upset you. If you could just tell me why that is, maybe we can find a way to work this out. I miss you, so does the rest of the group."

She pondered this and then she huffed out a short breath. She turned in the swing so she was facing me, legs pulled up and crossed.

"It's just everything all at once Lux. I know you've been doing this for years but, I guess I just figured you'd grow out of it eventually. I thought you'd grow up, get a grip, get your life together and actually be with one person."

I had the beginnings of a panic attack going after she said those words. My eyes were glued to her as she spoke and I hoped she hadn't decided to make me a project for domestication. I let out a barely audible sigh when she shook her head and looked away from me. Her gaze swept out over the yard before she spoke again.

"It's just hard watching you do this week after week and knowing that there's no remorse. It seems like there's no understanding or concern for what you might be doing to these girls, what kind of mess you're leaving them."

She looked back to me and I thought I was beginning to understand.

"Court..."

"I'm not done, Lux. It was always bad enough when it was just you. I mean, we got a few laughs out of it here and there and some of your stories were amazing. We all thought you were something else when we were younger, in high school this was cool. Back then you were cool. Now it's just sad and lonely and, well, now you have James doing it too. She has the charm to pull it off, sure, but didn't you stop to think that you might be ruining her for some perfect girl? That there's someone out there just right for her and now you've ruined that, ruined her..."

Of course I hadn't thought about it. My mind didn't work in those ways. The realm of relationships and girlfriends and forever and all of those things was foreign to me.

"No, I hadn't considered that. I wouldn't have though would I? I mean, have I ever considered relationships? Connections? Any of it?"

"I don't know, I guess not."

"I respect exactly one relationship. Zara and Dani's, because they're my friends, but I've slept with both of them! I know this lifestyle I've allowed myself to make a habit of is a little destructive but, it's me, it's all I know. As for James, well... She wanted this, she asked me to help her. Something tells me she probably would have figured it out on her own eventually, she barely needed my help, honestly."

Courtney's eyes misted over and her cheeks flushed. Suddenly I understood what might be happening.

"Do you like James?"

I asked the question softly, staring right at her as the words left my mouth. She looked down at her folded hands and nodded ever so slightly. No wonder she had laid into me, it didn't have so much to do with my lifestyle. It had to do with the fact I had brought James into it.

"No wonder you bit my head off. Look, do you want me to talk to James?"

"No, Lux, please don't, it'll just embarrass me."

"Well, now that we have that shit resolved, will you start hanging out with us again?"

"It's not resolved, Lux, not at all. That was half of it, sure but, not everything."

I tried to accept there being more than one reason she exploded on me that night. Instead, all I could think was 'wonderful, this will not be getting any better any time soon'. After her first bombshell and my thought process, I didn't know what the hell to expect.

"Well, what's the rest, if I know, I can fix it."

She shook her head and looked at me like I was clueless, which, at the moment, I really felt like I was.

"I can't tell you. I wish I could, okay, it would make all of this so much easier but, I just can't."

"Why?"

"Because while I'm the one that reacted and took offense about it, it isn't my issue to discuss, Lux."

"Then tell me who and I'll go discuss it."

She shook her head again and I started to think the conversation was a dead end. I dropped the subject and went for another.

"Okay, well then what do I need to do for you to come back to the group? Everyone misses you."

"Quit sleeping around... Or stop showing up."

Wow, she had decided to lay some pretty heavy baggage on me. I gaped at her.

"Wow. Damn, okay... Well, starting tomorrow night I won't be there then. I'll go elsewhere."

She shook her head as if to convey that even though it had been offered as an option, I had made the wrong choice. I felt irritation beginning to spark deep inside myself. I had been in my current state of being, doing what I was doing, for years. I was fourteen when it began and it had remained fairly steady ever since. I figured after fourteen years, my friends should be used to my escapades. Asking me to change because it was suddenly awkward for them was ridiculous.

"Whatever, look I'm trying to fix this shit okay? I just don't know what the fuck you expect from me!"

I had slipped from irritated to pissed off as she sat there and looked at me like I was some kind of monster.

"I would hope that you would expect a little better from, and for, yourself Lux."

"Fuck! Look, I get that your church centered mind might find the things I do damnable but I'm not you Courtney. This is who I am and I'm sorry if that's suddenly not good enough for you, okay? I can't deal with this shit right now."

She stared at me, apparently stunned. She appeared to be having some trouble forming words so I took the opportunity to leave. I walked away from her. She sat there in what I assumed to be silent shock. What had transpired counted as only the second or third such outburst she'd ever heard from me. I needed some distance between us and I needed it fast. Not to mention I had the urge to go home with someone and work off some of this irritation.

I didn't bother going back to the bar. I could still manage to salvage something from the night but was intent on doing it without the company of my friends. I wondered how many of them agreed with Courtney about my behavior but shrugged it off. I couldn't venture down the road those thoughts led to, not tonight, not without all of them present to defend themselves. It would have to wait.

I ducked into the first place with a promising air about it. I hit the bar and had a drink in hand in a matter of a few minutes. I slammed the first and ordered a second, picking it up and heading out onto the floor to do some hunting. It only took me a few seconds to find what I was looking for. A predatory grin worked its way across my face as I wound my way through the crowd toward her.

I had decided to make my life easy for once. The place I had ducked into happened to be a predominantly queer bar. I approached a small group of girls gathered near the pool tables. There were four of them total chatting and laughing. They looked barely legal, a couple possibly too young to be in the bar. I placed the oldest at about twenty-two, a whole six years younger than me. I could definitely live with the age gap. I stepped up to the table they were occupying about the time they split up to play a team game.

I would have gone for any of them but one girl caught my eye once they were under the brighter lights. She was shorter than me, maybe five-foot-three, slim but toned if the bare section of stomach she was showing off was any indication. She had red hair, the natural kind, not the bottle type and appeared to have green eyes. I waited for her to finish her shot, knowing there would be three more before she was up again. Once she'd gone I stepped up beside her and leaned next to her at the empty table she was propped against.

She looked at me with a shocked expression but then grinned when I shifted my gaze over onto her. I had to reassess her age once I got a good look. She probably shouldn't even be in this place, fake IDs are everywhere these days. I put her at the literal barely legal mark, eighteen, maybe nineteen at best. Oh well, I wasn't about to back out, not when she was looking at me like she was. The game was on.

"Hi."

She spoke first and I flashed a half-smile at her before offering her a nod in return to her greeting.

"I'm Sara."

Sara, easy to remember, not that I cared, I never bothered with names, too many chances to make mistakes and use the wrong one.

"Hi Sara, I'm Lux."

I reached over for her hand and she gave it to me, blushing when her skin met mine. I let the half-smile on my face slip into a full one. It made her own smile falter and forced her to take a sharp breath in. Someone told me once that smile had an effect on people. Other women seemed to be tripped up by it and I used it as a weapon.

"So, any plans after you leave here, Sara?"

She shook her head, still holding onto my hand and I didn't bother letting go. Instead I used the hand to tug her closer and put my lips right against her ear.

"Want to get out of here?"

She let out the faintest hint of a whimper. Had her own lips not been right against my ear, I might have missed it. I adopted a cocky smirk when she nodded against my cheek.

"Guys I... I'll see you later, okay?"

She offered the words over her shoulder to her friends without actually looking at them, and then grabbed her jacket. She tugged it on without waiting for a response and I dropped my arm across her shoulders. We walked out of the bar together and hailed a cab. She gave the driver the address and by the time he pulled away from the curb she was practically in my lap. Our lips had connected, the kiss hard and deep. We didn't come up for air until the cab stopped in front of the Marriot downtown.

I tossed some money at the driver as we exited. We rushed into the building then waited impatiently for the elevator. Once it arrived we stepped in, she hit the button for the top floor and the car began to move. I was done waiting. I had been off my game for almost a week and I was feeling really pent up. I needed to fix it, pronto. I reached over and hit the emergency stop, bringing the elevator car to a halt between floors two and three.

When I turned back to Sara she looked shocked but it passed a moment later, replaced by confusion. She glanced at the emergency stop and then back to me. I decided I wasn't going to try and explain. I yanked her shirt over her head and dropped it to the floor. That seemed to explain everything. By the time I had her against the side of the box she was back in and proved she was okay skipping the wait as well.

I made quick work of her bra. As I dropped it on her shirt I pressed my right thigh between her legs, parting them to give space to work my magic. She had opted for a skirt despite the weather. The rough denim of my jeans made contact between her legs, ripping a gasp from her. That was all I'd needed to hear. One of the many sounds my ears had missed so much and it flipped me into overdrive.

My head dipped down so I could nip at her neck and she let out a soft moan in response to my efforts. I continued down and the sound she made when my tongue met her exposed and already erect nipple was like music to my ears. I grinned against her flesh and let my hand work its way up under her skirt. I expelled a sharp breath when I realized why she had reacted so intensely to the contact of my leg between hers. She had gone commando, I loved it when they opted out of underwear. I allowed two short breaths to marvel at how I managed to find these girls before I continued. My fingers edged along her lips, picking up moisture as they moved. She was already wet but then, so was I.

I couldn't help but tease her just a little before my fingers slipped between her lips and found her clit. She had finally put her hands to work, heading south on my body and intent. The motion halted suddenly as her head fell back against the polished wall. Her eyes fluttered closed and I used the pause to move my mouth to her other nipple. I started slow circles over her clit as my tongue regained contact. She shivered against me, found her ability to control her hands and eased them down my body again.

Her breathing sounded somewhat ragged to my ears as she reached the button on my jeans. It took her three tries to work it open then several frustrated tugs to pull down my zipper. I tried to contain the smug smile claiming my face, but it won. Thankfully my face was still planted firmly against her perfect chest. Her hand found its way between our bodies and her fingers slipped under the elastic of my black boy shorts.

The tip of her middle finger found its mark seconds later. In four short flicks she halted everything my own hand was doing up her skirt. Shit this girl knew what she was doing. I recovered enough to return to my rhythm as she found her own against my already overly sensitive nub. I slid my hand down further, pressing two fingers into her. I knew she was wet enough to take them both deep and fast without any further warmup. She leaned her head against the side of my neck and let out a moan. I tingled.

As she panted against the soft spot near my collarbone, her warm breath brushed in quick bursts over my already flushed skin. Her free hand tangled into my hair and her right leg came up to my hip. She wrapped her calf part way around my waist. I picked up a rhythm that had me pushing hard and fast into her over and over again, the pad of my thumb keeping pace against her clit.

She pushed her hand deeper into my jeans, finding me more than ready for her. She wasted no time as slid two fingers into me showing no hesitation. She definitely wasn't new to this rodeo and I was thankful for it. I needed more than a fumbling encounter with a first timer. I curled my fingers inside her with each stroke out. Fingertips brushed against her g-spot with each stroke and she muttered obscenities. God was mentioned several times as well.

I wondered if she spoke to Him regularly or if I was receiving a special kind of prayer. She matched my pace stroke for stroke and mirrored the movements of my fingers. My mouth was forced from her left breast as a breathy 'oh fuck' tore from my lips. I leaned against her shoulder, my own breathing almost as ragged as hers. I decided to play dirty and bit down on her collarbone. Apparently she liked a little pain with her pleasure because it pushed her over the edge.

She threw her head back against the wall of the elevator, screaming into the small space. Her entire body convulsed and tightened around my fingers and my hip as she came. The sound of her scream dragged me right along behind her. I let my own muffled cry loose against her shoulder seconds later. Thankfully she seemed to think like I did. Despite the fact we had both climaxed, neither of us stopped. We pushed for the other to peak again, refusing to let it end so soon.

I pressed her into a rough kiss, my tongue pushing past her lips and taking control. I left no room for hesitation or a fight, simply demanding she give in to me. At the contact she pressed in closer and I pushed into her hard, holding my fingers as deep as they could go. Forever thankful for my forearm conditioning, I fluttered the tips of my fingers in a fast rhythm inside her. At the same time my tongue caressed the roof of her mouth. I was delighted when the combined sensations pushed her over the edge again.

She ripped away from my lips so she could scream again. I loved that sound. It combined with her mirrored finger action inside my body. She raked her nails hard down my back under my shirt. I couldn't hold back. I came again, pressing her hard against the wall as sparks and heat exploded through my body. A rush of intense twitches and shivers rippled through me for several seconds and my ears were ringing.

I leaned against her, both of our bodies shuddering with aftershocks for a couple minutes. The wall propped us up as we each attempted to catch our breath. When we could breathe again and had some chance of moving without falling over, she moved. She retrieved her bra and shirt, pulled them on and ran her fingers through her hair as the elevator started moving again. I laughed, fumbled a few times and barely got the zipper up on my jeans before we reached the right floor and the doors opened.

We stepped out as I ran my fingers through my hair to try and fix it, thankful it was short. Sex hair and bed head worked at lengths similar to mine. She led me to her room, opened the door and waved me inside. The door closed behind me with a soft thump against the jam. I heard the click of the lock and whirled to face her. My pride, not to mention my currently ravenous libido, wasn't about to let her recover for too long before starting again.

What we'd done in the elevator was not nearly enough. I'd caught the scent of her on my fingers. I needed to taste her. I wouldn't be happy until she was delirious and couldn't walk for hours. She was back out of her shirt and bra within the space of two breaths. Now we were safe behind a real door so I pulled off her skirt and shoes as well. I dropped them on the floor with the other clothes.

She seemed to register that I had stayed completely clothed in the elevator. With a sexy smirk on her face, helped me out of everything I had on. She added them to the pile and we didn't give them another thought. I shot her a wicked grin, putting the beginnings of a worried expression on her features. I couldn't have the look in place for long so I picked her up and literally tossed her onto the bed. I was stronger than I looked and she let out a yelp when she bounced twice.

She giggled when the movement stopped, actually giggled. It was kind of cute and made me chuckle wondering if I could cause it again. She slid up the bed and settled against the headboard as the giggles ceased. The look she gave me couldn't be labeled as cute by any means and it cut off all function in my brain for about ten seconds. I'd seen that look dozens of times over the years and it was pure need. She wanted me and it was showing. I liked the way it made me feel.

Her previously bright green eyes were deep, forest green when they swept my naked body. I could almost feel the heat against my skin. Her gaze smoldered its way right through me. I shivered. Damn this girl was something and I intended to make sure she would remember me. I had to be well on my way there already. I let my eyes wander uninhibited over her naked body. I couldn't put my finger on when exactly the clean shaven look had become popular but I thanked whoever happened to be listening for the phenomenon.

My smile widened as I crawled onto the bed and between her legs, using my arms to spread them for me. I eased my body down until my lips were only inches from her wet core. I should have gotten right to it and not teased the poor girl any further but I couldn't help myself. I ran the tip of my tongue from the bottom of her slit all the way to the top. I broke contact long enough to savor the taste then probed lightly between her lips to flick over her clit.

I only did it once then leaned away again, putting about three inches between her glistening skin and my lips. She let out a soft moan, trailed by a whimper when contact was lost and pressed back against the headboard. She moved one hand up to hold onto the solid wood, apparently preparing herself for what was to come. She reached for me with the other, the needy tremor of the repeated whimper finding my ears. I knew what she wanted and I could very easily move back to where I'd been and let her have it.

I was in a mood though and I felt the need to push her further. I eased her legs further apart, exposing more of her sensitive flesh to me. I pursed my lips and pushed out a gentle stream of breath against the wetness between her legs. She whined, rolling her hips against the bed as her eyes met mine, holding my gaze. She must have read what I was after in my expression because she gave me what I wanted.

"Please."

The word was barely more than a whisper, breathy and filled with a pleading tone that made my breath catch. I considered really making her beg then realized how badly I wanted her and changed my mind. I shifted up again, close enough for her to reach me and she twisted her fingers into my hair. She pulled hard and an involuntary moan fell free of me as I shivered. I couldn't for the life of me figure out why they always wanted to pull my hair. I loved the way it felt.

The yank had an instant effect in the form of my mouth coming into full contact with her. I spent a few minutes praising her clit with my tongue, flicking, massaging, and circling. I waited until she was moaning and writhing under me to let my fingers push into her and find her center. She had gotten so worked up I eased three fingers inside her without much resistance. It took less than a minute of brushing and pressing against her heat for her to slam her shoulders back against the headboard. She threw her head back, screaming her climax to the ceiling.

She tapped my head to let me know her muscles needed a break so I slipped my fingers out of her. I slid backwards until my feet could hit the floor then stood up. I grinned at her as I went for my clothes, seeing her already collapsing into the bed. Her eyes were barely open but a huge smile had painted its way onto her face. My work with her was done so I used one of the hand towels in the bathroom to wipe my face and washed my hands. Cleaned up, I gathered my clothes, got dressed and made a swift, silent exit.

I had about three minutes to think while I was standing outside the hotel. My phone in my hand, I stared at the screen and wondered if maybe Courtney was right. Granted I had met this particular girl in a gay bar but she couldn't have been more than nineteen once I'd gotten a good look at her. She had been out with her friends, having a good time. I had insinuated myself into their group and poured on the sexy predator façade perfected over the years. I doubted she had gone into the place looking for someone like me and now she would wake up alone.

She was staying in a hotel so I could assume she didn't live in the area and was on vacation or did live in the area and was trying to escape something. A few weeks ago I would have told myself it didn't matter. Either way I had helped out. Either she'd had a great vacation experience and now had a crazy story to tell or I'd helped her take her mind off of her problems for a while. Now I felt like a total bitch and it made me crave a shower and maybe a little soul searching. Maybe a lot of soul searching.

I heaved a sigh, unlocked my phone screen and called Angel. It was a safe bet she and James were the least likely to judge me for the incident. However, James might be busy with someone so Angel was first choice. She answered on the second ring and the noise in the background let me know they were in the car.

"Hey! Where have you been, we've been worried about you!"

"Sorry. I just needed a walk and, I'll explain everything later I promise. Where are you guys?"

"Just left the bar we were at. Where are you?"

I told her and she told me to hang tight and they would be there to get me in a couple minutes. I sat on a concrete parking stop to wait. Thankfully I didn't have much time with my thoughts before they pulled up and I hopped in the front passenger seat. A quick glance told me Zara and Dani had opted to sit together in the backseat and James was nowhere to be found. I shook my head as I mentally reprimanded myself, Courtney's voice in my head. I settled back into the seat, letting myself think about her words and giving in to the fact she was right.

There was a damn good chance I had ruined James for ever being in a real relationship with anyone. Gods knew I was a waste of time when relationships were concerned. I didn't think I had even retained the ability to remember a girl's name once I walked out her door. It hit me hard exactly how sad it sounded. I tamped the thoughts down and tried to ignore them. I was back with my friends so I needed to stop being lame.

I kept quiet for the drive but at least appeared to be listening. I managed to catch bits and pieces of the conversation going on around me. None of it really stuck though and I zoned out for several comments and ended up completely lost. Eventually Angel dropped Zara and Dani off at their place and then headed toward our house, not speaking, letting me decide when I was ready to talk.

"Angel?"

"Yeah honey."

"Am I completely hopeless? I mean, am I a terrible friend?"

"What? How can you even ask that?"

"Just answer me, please. And be honest with me, I need it right now."

"No, Lux, you are not a terrible friend. You're actually a really good friend, if not a bit distracted frequently. You're always there for any one of us that needs you."

I nodded and let the words settle in and then the car fell back into silence, comfortable silence, but silence all the same. It stayed quiet for five full miles before I ventured an attempt at speaking again.

"I went to talk to Court tonight."

"Oh yeah? And?"

"And we got into a fight."

"About what?"

"Me mostly, and my behavior, the way I am, the way I treat people."

"The way you treat people? What's that mean?"

"She says I don't care about anyone but myself and that I've been using these girls, honestly, I'm starting to think she's right. I mean, you heard her last week when we were out."

"I know and I still can't believe she said that shit. She's getting a little full of herself lately and... Ugh, oh my god, Lux. Don't even listen to her. I don't know where she pulled that from but she's got some nerve. It's really no wonder she's been avoiding us."

"Not *us* Angel... Me."

"Huh?"

"She's avoiding me, not the group. Actually, she kinda told me that if I stop going out with you guys she'll start coming again. So I told her that tonight was it, I'd figure something else out."

"You did what? No... No, I don't think so. I'm not going to start letting Courtney dictate who can and can't be in this group. She's getting a little too high and mighty for me and I'm tired of it."

"Just drop it, Angel, seriously. She said some things that made sense and actually made a confession that made me feel like a first rate asshole. I've accepted that I'm kinda broken and I screw with people. I just think I might be too far gone to change."

Angel gave me the look she would get sometimes. It's the one that says 'I don't care if it's a secret, I'm your best friend and you will tell me'. I resisted as long as I could but in the end I caved in and told her everything Courtney had said.

CHAPTER FOUR

Saturday, February 21ˢᵗ, 2009 – San Tan Valley, Arizona
Angel had taken the news as well as I could expect and had sworn she wouldn't say anything to our group. I got an extra promise she would zip it around James and we made the rest of the trip home in silence. She seemed like she had expected something else, some other news. We made it to the house and then went our separate ways for the night. Alone and running at full steam meant another night staring at my ceiling. It took me hours to settle my brain and get rid of the things Court had said enough to sleep.

I grumbled and rubbed at my eyes, which felt like sandpaper had been stapled to the insides of my eyelids. They finally watered and the gritty feeling eased away so I was able to open my eyes. Sort of. What greeted me was the mid-morning sun, bright, golden and far too cheery for my tastes. I felt anything but cheery. All the sun managed to do was coax a growl out of me as I rolled over and pulled the blanket over my head. I lifted the corner enough to get one unfocused eye on the clock and grumbled a string of profanity. James would be waking me up soon.

I was so ready for the Saturday shifts to be over. I was considering telling Mr. Kane where to shove it and calling out of work for the day. I was in the middle of figuring out what I could tell him, how I would get myself out of this day when there was a knock on my door. I didn't even need to hear the voice from the other side to know who it was and what she wanted.

"Hey Lux, time to get ready for work. Let's go."

I growled at her, threw the covers back so I could roll out of bed and shuffled to the bathroom. I showered on autopilot and then managed to walk rather than shuffle back to my room. I was still dripping and not couldn't be bothered with a towel, everyone in the house had seen me naked. I shut the bedroom door and leaned back against it with a heavy sigh. Even after a shower I was half asleep and needed another couple hours in bed.

I finally pushed away from the door to get dressed for the day. Once I was in my black slacks and a pale yellow shirt I tugged on my shoes and belt. Then it was back in the bathroom to tame my hair. All accomplished I wandered into the kitchen where the sounds of breakfast being made were punctuated by laughter. As I crossed into the room I couldn't help but notice Rascal was missing yet again. I wasn't about to ask and I shoved the feeling the possibilities brought up aside before anyone noticed I was being weird.

"Hey guys."

"Well good morning sunshine. About time you grace us with your presence."

Even after twenty-four years as her friend I had no clue how Angel could be so damn chipper in the morning. I didn't have it in me, no questioning that fact, morning and I weren't on speaking terms. I flipped her off for daring to be perky in my presence at eight in the morning. She laughed and stuck her tongue out at me then turned back to making breakfast. She chatted away with James like she'd been up for hours. I slid into one of the dining chairs and stared silently at the tabletop, letting them talk around me until food was done cooking.

They joined me at the table and Angel set a plate in front of me. I stared at it for longer than I probably should have. I pushed it away a couple inches before letting out a small sigh.

"Oh just eat it, grumpy. A little breakfast won't kill you, I promise."

"Sorry, Angel. I know you take time out of your day to make sure we eat in the morning. I'm just a little out of it today."

She gave me a smirk and a raised eyebrow. I knew the look was for my use of 'today' in my last sentence. I watched her and knew she was counting the number of mornings I had actually been so 'out of it' recently. I hated the damn knowing look she had been giving me, like she knew what was going on in my head. She probably knew exactly what had been bothering me, best friends are like that. They get in your head and organize things, dig through drawers and move shit around. Sometimes she knew me better than I knew myself.

I looked away from her, glad James was already eating and seemed to be completely oblivious to the exchange. I pulled my plate back over and dug in. I managed to finish the food Angel had made without tasting much of it and then headed out for work. I spent the drive giving myself a pep talk and attempting to get excited about the whole ordeal. It didn't work.

Thankfully the day was filled with tasks which were easy to work on while I was simultaneously half asleep and only half paying attention. I'd had a sudden onset of serious ADD. I was in need of a night out and I didn't even care if my friends were going. I wanted a break from it all. I had been off and out of it for longer than I liked and I needed to feel like myself again, so I decided I was heading out alone.

I relived the night before once or twice, reconsidering my path for the night each round. Every time I talked myself back into the original plan. I needed to get back to being me. To hell with how Courtney felt about my behavior. She had no right to tell me how to live my life, no one did. I was twenty-eight and would do as I pleased. I would go out and I would do exactly as I had always done and not feel bad about it. If the girls worried or wanted to join me, they would call or text. I would gladly tell them where I was, until then, it was me and the lovely ladies of the greater Phoenix metro area.

As I stepped into the darkened room, lights flashing around me, bodies packed almost from wall to wall, I actually worked up a smile. The pounding of the bass cleared my mind of everything. I was thankful for the mental silence even if it turned out to be fleeting. Thoughts freshly purged, mind back on track, I started a scan of the room as I made for the bar. It took me a few minutes to get close enough to order anything but I finally walked away with a drink in hand. I took a sip of the Captain and Coke, what I was sure would be the first glass of many for the night and grinned at the mass of bodies.

I wouldn't let my brain get in the way tonight. I told myself I was done analyzing my own thoughts and finding reasons to pick apart my own behavior. It made me act off my normal center and kept me moody. It was time to start being my charming if not slightly over-sexed self again. More than time as a matter-of-fact. I'd slipped back into my pattern the night before and it had felt amazing. I closed my eyes and let my thoughts wander back to the hotel room and... What the hell was her name? I couldn't remember but I decided I didn't care.

After two drinks and at least four laps of the room I was still unsure if there was anyone I wanted to put my time into. Sure it was only one night, and actually more like a couple hours, but my time and efforts were still valuable. At least I was telling myself as much so I wouldn't leave with any random drunk girl. I decided I needed a break and slipped out the door and onto the sidewalk to have a cigarette. I tapped one out of the pack, lit it and took the first drag. The rough burn of it hit my lungs and a small smile turned up the corners of my lips.

A little voice deep inside me said I should quit. It was a terrible habit and really bad for me, but it was one of those things I couldn't seem to shake off. I made my way to the parking lot to finish the smoke. I grabbed some real estate near my car. I considered if it would once again end up spending the night right where it was. The thought made my grin widen as I remembered why I was out, what I was after and what I'd shown up at this club to do.

I finished the cigarette, flicked the butt to the pavement and stomped it out before I made my way back inside. I was more determined now than I had been before. I figured a shot would help me focus and went to the bar to order one. I downed it then turned on the packed room again. I seemed to be back in my element, which felt nice in a weird and probably twisted way. It didn't take me long to make a choice, giving myself a bit of a challenge this time around.

It ended up taking a vodka and cranberry, a shot of tequila and two dances to get my pick out the door. Not too bad, I'd had tougher pick-ups. We were both far too tipsy to drive so we called for a ride. Once we were in the car, she gave the address for her place. Logistics handled we fell into a heated make-out session in the backseat. We practically tripped over each other getting out of the car as soon as it stopped. I made sure I tossed some money at the driver then we made our way into the apartment. She lived on the ground floor, thankfully and appeared to live alone.

Well, I hoped she did since she started pulling both our clothes off right there in the living room. When her bra hit the floor, I gave up caring if she had roommates and shut out the rest of my surroundings. I was back in my element and I wasn't about to get distracted and disappoint. I never had and I wouldn't be starting tonight. I might leave them wondering when I'd slipped out but I never left them wanting. Call it a point of pride. We made quick work of the rest of our clothes, helping each other out of them and then I was on my back on the couch.

I had learned a few things over the years, things which had been picked up after dozens of hook-ups. Most girls will fall into bed with another female given the right mindset – or enough alcohol - this girl was a different kind though. She was surprisingly assertive, damn near dominating. I almost bothered to wonder if she'd done this before but then remembered I didn't care. Before I had the chance to reconsider the thought she was straddling me. One hand tangled in my hair, her tongue practically down my throat.

She didn't have much in her corner for tact but damn she could kiss and I was willing to be the submissive one. Before I could register much she had her free hand between our bodies and a shudder rippled over me as one fingertip connected with my clit. Damn, she didn't waste any time, I wasn't about to complain though. It averaged out to about one time in every three or four I actually got anything out of these nights. Any time I got one who was willing to give before she got I would ride it out.

Some things were clear within a matter of half a dozen heartbeats. One - this girl knew what the hell she was doing, and two - my body was responding to it. There had been almost no foreplay but I realized I didn't even need it. Apparently having a pretty girl take charge was the same thing, interchangeable. I heard a stifled moan and realized I had made the sound. I tightened my grip on the edge of the couch cushion with one hand and tangled the other in her hair. She got my breathing to the point where I had to tear my lips from hers to get a few harsh, ragged breaths into my protesting lungs.

She gave me the space of four deep breaths to fill my lungs and then she was back in action. She moved to slide her finger down off my clit which made me pout, not something I was proud of but it happened. She put the smile right back in place a moment later when she completely buried two fingers into me in one quick thrust. My back arched up off the couch and I let out a loud moan. She jerked my head to one side using the handful of my hair she was still holding and ran her tongue up my neck. I had a split second to wonder who had picked whom up in the club before she started moving.

Her fingers slid out and then pushed back in, curling then

ending in a slight twisting motion on each stroke. I shuddered hard and started moving my hips with her rhythm, meeting each stroke. The contact at the end of each thrust forced her fingers as deep as they could possibly go. It hurt and I knew I would be sore and bruised in the morning but I loved it. The stinging ache made me writhe under her and elicited a series of moans from me.

The orgasm hit me with no warning, no tingle, no pressure, and no build-up. Only a sudden tensing of muscles which slammed the air from my lungs and arched my back pressing me against her as I bit back a loud cry. She gave the aftershocks time to run their course, letting my muscles begin to relax then eased her fingers from me and released my hair. I was sore, tingling from head to toe and covered in a thin layer of sweat that shimmered in the moonlight bleeding through the front window.

I laid there stunned, completely unable to move, not wanting to try anyway. I sucked in a slow, deep breath, took in the delicious new kind of tingle telling me my muscles would be working again soon. I flexed my fingers and toes finding I was achy but able to move so I shifted one hand to her hip. I broke out in a rather wicked grin and looked up at her, one eyebrow quirked. She smirked at me, apparently having some idea what was coming and started to sit up so I could move.

I let her make it about halfway before I tightened my grip on her hair and hip both. I turned her, moving as I did and straddled her across my lap. Her back pressed against my chest, head tilted back to rest on my shoulder. Her breath caught at the force I put behind the move and then again when my right hand slipped down her stomach. My middle finger found her clit without any hesitation and she gasped. Initial contact made, I decided to have a little fun, pay her back for her lack of foreplay with an abundance of it.

I kept my movements slow, teasing, wanting to make her beg for more. When I was sixteen I had discovered a particular talent for patience when I was on the giving end of my encounters. It served me well when I had nights like this one ~ Nights when I needed to hear someone beg, plead with me to give them what they wanted. I had perfected the technique over the course of the twelve years since my sweet sixteen and I aimed to use it on, whatever her name was. It didn't take me long to have her panting and whimpering at me. I refused to be rushed, keeping my pace slow and my pressure steady, enough to drive her crazy but not let her peak.

"Stop teasing me, dammit."

The words were breathy and barely louder than a whisper, about all she could manage right then if I had to guess. It was cute how she tried to be commanding when the very tone and pitch in her voice already held the ghosted whimper of pleading. I wasn't about to give in so easily and rather than obliging and giving her what she wanted I leaned in and ran my tongue down her neck and over her shoulder. She shuddered hard, let out a soft moan and rolled her hips against my hand, asking me again to stop teasing her, no words needed.

I grinned against her skin and then, brushing my lips up to the soft spot right at the top of her shoulder, I bit down. Not hard enough to break skin but it would definitely leave a mark, something to remember me by. She cried out, stifling the sound by biting down on her bottom lip and pushed her hips hard against my fingers making me bite back a chuckle.

"Did you want something, then?"

I had slipped into being an asshole and I knew it, but I wanted her to say it, wanted to hear her ask me for what she wanted, beg for what she needed from me.

"God I... Shit... So hate you... Oh fuck... Right now... Dammit... Fuck me. Please... Please..."

The last please was whimpered at me, needy, wanting and exactly what I'd been after. I needed like she did, only my desire had been for something other than release. She'd suffered enough and I gave her what she wanted. In one fluid move I was off the couch and had her planted on her hands and knees on it as I positioned myself behind her. My left arm slipped around her waist, my fingertip finding her clit again, harder this time, no longer interested in teasing her. My right hand went to work, two fingers sliding into her quickly. She shivered out a curse and lay her head on the arm of the couch.

Apparently she had enjoyed my teasing, she was soaking wet and I easily managed to add a third finger after two or three thrusts. The extra pressure forced a moan from her she didn't even attempt to stop and I smiled as I picked up a steady but deep and hard pace. I used my left arm to pin her close against my lower body. Her movements helped to force my fingers deeper. It couldn't have been more than two minutes before the telltale signs began. Her breaths shortened, becoming ragged, harsh.

Her moans and whimpers became frantic as her muscles twitched. The minor contractions gripped my fingers with each tremor. I leaned over her and traced my tongue up her spine and it worked like pulling a trigger. All at once she exploded, her upper body coming up away from the couch. I barely managed to move with her but spared my nose from being broken. She pressed her back against my chest and tensed up against me. She reached back with both hands to hold onto me, nails of one digging into my hip as fingers of the other gripped the back of my neck.

Her head fell back against my shoulder, her scream echoed through the room and I was sure it had alerted the neighbors of our activities. More shocking was my reaction to it all. The combination of her unhindered climax and the pressure of her fingers locked against my skin sent another orgasm rocking through me. I clamped my teeth down on the soft skin right below her ear, intending to leave my mark with this one. She cried out and it sounded so far from a reaction to pain I had to assume she was enjoying herself. My body shuddered several times then relaxed and I released her skin from between my teeth and held her tight against me.

She started to come down. I considered letting her. The consideration lasted about three seconds before I smirked to myself and dismissed the idea. I had a reputation to think about and I couldn't leave her on the one, even if it had been intense. I gave her long enough to be able to move so I could slip out from behind her. I shifted around in front and laid her back against the opposite arm of the couch. I dropped down between her legs, small shivering convulsions still trickling through her as her climax ebbed away and I grinned up at her.

It appeared she suddenly realized what was happening and went wide eyed. She opened her mouth, about to say something before my head dropped and my tongue darted out against her clit. She jerked, any thoughts of protest torn from her lips with the action. She writhed under my hands as they wrapped around her thighs. I quirked an eyebrow and moved my tongue down. I gave her one long, slow lick between her lips and then probe into her still quivering opening.

Her head dropped back against the arm of the couch as she let out a moan. I had always loved being with vocal women and she was an extreme case. It was like a high I never wanted to come down off of. I licked at her before returning my tongue to her clit. I fell into a rhythm as my fingers slipped inside her again, finding her even wetter than she had been. I wasn't quite sure how it was possible but who was I to argue?

She hadn't come down completely from her first climax and the second one seemed to hit before I'd even gotten started. A curl of my fingers, a few rough flicks of fingertips against her already over-stimulated g-spot. Her muscles jumped and twitched then she came again. Hard. The scream that ripped from her made the first seem like she'd been faking it. I registered the word the scream had formed and was stunned she had remembered my name. It sounded good screamed.

I removed myself from on top of her and settled in sitting at the other end of her couch, watching her come down. A slow smile spread across her face, her eyes closed and her breathing still hard. I couldn't help but allow myself a smug smile. Since I was sitting there and she wasn't paying attention I finally took a better look at her. She was about five-foot-six with black hair and, from what I could remember, light eyes, though my brain couldn't settle on blue or green.

As she eased those eyes open after a couple minutes they had darkened to an alarming shade of deep forest green with thick lashes, settled under perfectly-sculpted brows. She was cute, no doubt about it, but then, they usually were. Cute wouldn't keep me around for longer than I needed to completely recover and get dressed.

"So, this is the part where you get dressed, tell me it's been fun but you have shit to do and it's complicated and say you'll see me around, right?"

Damn, chick had the song and dance down. I couldn't help but wonder if she'd been through this all before even if the words were soft, slightly breathy and held no hints of reproach.

"I take it this isn't your first time through this, then?"

She laughed and shook her head then slipped off the couch and gathered up her clothes, putting them back on as she retrieved each piece.

"Yeah, I kinda figured you didn't remember me. That's okay, I wasn't delusional enough to think you would."

I was confused and I was sure it showed across my face as I quirked a brow at her and waited for an explanation.

"We went through this same song and dance three years ago. I was only eighteen then, you picked me up at Pride."

My brow furrowed until my brain kicked in and I realized I had seen those eyes before. She was right, we'd been in this position once before tonight.

"Shit."

"It's okay, I know you don't usually repeat girls, at least that's what I've heard. But I already know not to expect anything from you. Here."

She tossed my clothes at me and I sat there stunned and unable to move. I tried to get my thoughts together so I could speak, say something, anything.

"Look, I..."

She silenced me by raising one hand and shook her head, a small laugh slipping from her lips.

"Don't bother, Lux. I didn't need an explanation then and I don't need one now. It was fun, now it's over. I'm okay with that."

She picked up her phone from the place on the floor it had landed when she'd thrown her pants. She tapped the screen a few times and then made a face at it.

"I do have to go pick up my drunk-ass girlfriend though so, show yourself out if you don't mind."

With the words hanging in the air she grabbed her keys, slipped on her shoes and was out the door before I could say anything in response. Had that actually happened to me? Wow, what were the odds of the player being played? I was impressed and totally appalled then found myself wondering if this was how girls felt when they woke up after my disappearing act. If it got even close I could openly admit it sucked.

I frowned to myself at the thought and then huffed, pushed off the couch and started putting my clothes on. I was out the door and walking through the chill of the night, several blocks from the girls' apartment when a thought occurred to me. There had been one thing I hadn't bothered to be freaked out or appalled at. The girl I'd had sex with less than ten minutes ago had a girlfriend. She had cheated on someone, with me. For the first time ever I wondered how many times it had happened over the years.

I had the time and quiet to wonder why it had never bothered me before and I didn't have a good answer. I had always told myself other people's relationships weren't my concern and staying faithful to their partner was their responsibility, not mine. I couldn't help how it made me think about Zara and Dani. I wondered how I would feel if someone like me stepped in the middle of their relationship during a moment of weakness. My heart clenched and my temper flared and I knew without any hesitation I would lose it if anyone like me ever happened to them. They were so perfect together I couldn't ever imagine them in any way other than a couple.

Anyone who would be sick, twisted and depraved enough to come between them was a total ass as far as I was concerned. Then I realized I'd probably been doing exactly that to other people's friends for years. I could have been destroying relationships for over a decade and hadn't cared. I had to stop and fight a wave of nausea that swept over me.

"Shit... What kind of bitch am I?"

I didn't have an answer other than the fact it must be a whole new level since I'd been doing it for so long, unchecked by my own moral compass. I fought my stomach under control and continued toward the parking lot where I'd left my car. Thankfully it wasn't terribly far, it had only seemed like a monumental hike when I was tipsy and had nothing but sex on my mind. Now I was glad for the cold air, the relative silence and the time to think. I probably should have done some deep thinking a long time ago.

I had so many things to work out, so much going on in my mind. I needed to start with what had slammed down on me earlier. I had to work my issues out, starting with giving a damn if someone I was trying to hook up with was actually dating someone. It would be easier said than done since I'd gotten in the habit of generally not giving a shit for so many years. I puffed out a heavy sigh, knowing completely reprogramming my brain wouldn't be easy. I made a promise to myself right then and there. I would do what I could to be more careful about who I went home with.

Of course the best I could do would be to ask, if they lied to me, well, then it wasn't on me, it was on them. I knew it was a loophole to make my life easier but I needed it in there somewhere, otherwise I would go crazy. It was settled by the time I made it back to my car. I would actually bother asking these girls if they were involved with someone. I had to keep myself from having more of these nights.

After the shock of what I had realized about myself and my behavior, I couldn't really handle any deeper self-understanding. I slid into the driver's seat of my car and started it, feeling completely sober after the mental and emotional beating I had given myself. I sat there in silence, shutting out the rest of what my mind wanted me to delve into and then turned the stereo on. I cranked the volume on some top forty pop song. I didn't care what it was, only that it was up too loud for me to think then I pulled out of the lot. As I turned toward home I was glad my radio tactic was working and I even caught myself singing along to some ridiculously peppy song that didn't match my mood at all.

By the time I made it home I felt minimally better and I turned down the volume on my radio so I wouldn't blow my ears the next time I got into the car, and then shut it off and headed inside. The house was dark and silent when I came in. Pippen, James' Shiba Inu, came padding up to me and nudged my calf so I knew she wasn't home otherwise he'd be in her room. I sighed and shook my head as everything Courtney had said to me came flooding to the surface and my guilt roared back to life. I really was a lost cause and I had dragged poor Jamie down with me into the pits of hell itself.

What made it worse was I wasn't sure I could fix it. She was out there right now, doing god knew what with god knew who. Sadly I was sure she was as uninterested as I had been before tonight about whether they were involved or not. She was also completely oblivious to how Court felt about her, which knotted my stomach up and made my heart hurt. I was ruining my friends and until the last few days I hadn't even cared. I didn't think I could get any more pathetic than I had become.

I flopped down on the couch, turned on my side facing the TV across the room and patted the spot next to my stomach. Pippen hopped up next to me and stretched out against my front. I wrapped an arm around him and buried my face in his cheek. He smelled like coconut and a sad, half sobbed chuckle slipped out. He must have been to the groomer earlier since the smell never lingered more than a day or so.

"I'm a total jackass, Pip."

I was fighting with a whole flood of emotions. Deep down I knew it was the only thing keeping me from breaking down, the fact they couldn't decide which should come out first. The dog sighed, turned his head and licked my nose before he shifted and nudged his muzzle under my chin. I almost smiled but then a warm, wet streak flowed over the bridge of my nose and fell to the fabric beneath me. I knew it was only the first of what I assumed would be many tears I cried before seeing morning.

"I know you love me buddy. About the only thing in this city that does I think."

Pippen was already snoring and I half-heartedly rolled my eyes at him. I tried to force the rest of the tears trying to fall back and settle in for the night. I didn't have it in me to bother getting up and walking the twenty or so feet to my bedroom. All I wanted to do was sleep the terrible night away. It had been emotional and involved far too much self-discovery for my liking. I tried to stay clear of delving into my own actions too deeply.

I did know I was getting too old to still be acting the way I did. I couldn't keep spending my weekends like I had been. If I was being honest I would admit I was this way because I was scared. I was downright terrified of actually having to care, of finding myself attached to someone who could hurt me. God help me I tried to lie to myself about it all, but if I did decide to be honest, there was the truth. The thought pierced through the floodgates I had so recently erected and the tears flowed freely. I couldn't stand crying, looking weak, but since no one was around I let the tears continue. Maybe a good cry would help.

I thought back to a time when I had allowed someone to have the kind of hold on my heart requiring trust and understanding. Only once had I ever let it happen. She had trampled my very soul. If only sleep would find me, but as usual lately it was being elusive. I hugged the dog for at least an hour, my mind on Heidi. I'd been as head over heels for her as any sixteen-year-old really could be and had even stopped hooking up with other girls to date her.

She was close to my idea of perfect. Beautiful, smart, funny, easy to talk to and sweet as could be, at least, in the beginning. She was a year older than me and I thought I was the luckiest girl in the world when she agreed to go out with me. Everything was going great and I was on cloud nine, until it all came crashing down around me. Seven months into our little high school romance I asked her to go to prom with me and her response was laughing in my face. I was crushed and the feeling only got worse as she proceeded to be brutally honest. She told me she had only been using me to kill time until the college guy she liked decided she was worth his time.

She spent the next several minutes explaining, in detail, why she would never be caught dead dating someone like me. As bad as the revelation was on its own, the fact she delivered in front of half the school was like twisting a knife in my gut. I remember wishing I could vanish into the crowd standing there. Some were gawking, others laughed at me for the tears running down my cheeks. She left me feeling used, hurt, defeated and worst of all, broken. No, not broken, completely emotionally shattered. I couldn't even muster up the words to defend myself or strike back at her. Thankfully, Angel had been there to do it for me and she ripped into her as I finally fled to hide.

I had fallen asleep somewhere during my trip down memory lane. Sadly, the dreams it conjured up were vivid and painful. They circled around Heidi and the hurt she had left me feeling, the broken heart I had spent the next few months nursing. It was like I was reliving it all over again and even in my sleep, my heart hurt for what I'd lost. Worse, what I'd thought I had and the ruse it had actually been. I woke up with a knot in my gut and a pain in my heart I hadn't felt in over a decade; one I had hoped I'd never feel again. Someone had found me sleeping on the couch at some point as I was now covered in the blanket that usually lived on the recliner and my shoes were on the floor under the coffee table.

As I finished waking up, I realized the house was silent and I glanced at the clock. It was almost noon and I groaned as I pushed myself up. One hand moved to rub my face and I decided I needed to shower and start my day. I wasn't sure where everyone was but the fact James hadn't been home when I came in meant she probably hadn't come back at all. I hadn't heard Angel moving around in the house this morning but that didn't really mean a whole lot. She was good at sneaking around me. She had done it a lot when we were teenagers so I could sleep in when I stayed over at her house. I had stopped checking if Rascal was home a few days back, always a little upset whether she was there or not.

I pushed up off the couch and shuffled zombie-style to the bathroom. I took my time showering, getting dressed to go nowhere and then plopped myself right back on the couch. I had decided I needed a big eventful day of watching some of my shows so I could clear the DVR. I flipped the TV on, hit the DVR menu and then sat there and stared at it, only half seeing it. I suddenly had no desire to catch up on any of my shows so I flipped the channel over to a music station and opened the ebook reader on my phone. I had always been a closet nerd and I read more than most people knew. At the moment I was on my sixth read through of *The Hobbit*.

CHAPTER FIVE

Saturday, March 14th, 2009 – Higley & Southern - Mesa, Arizona

James and I had finally finished the project which had us working Saturdays. We were glad to have a full weekend off for the first time in a couple months. The group, or most of it, was set up in the park down the street on the corner from Zara and Dani's house having a much needed gathering. We hadn't had a cookout in a few months so we were catching up. The weather was nice enough to lounge around in tee shirts without baking to death in the sun. Summer always came far too soon in Arizona and tended to hang around longer than absolutely necessary.

The day was somewhere in the seventies. I leaned back in the lawn chair I had taken over and closed my eyes. I had been trying to keep my mind clear of all the things which had been bouncing around in it the last few weeks, for today at least. I needed a break from trying to figure it all out, my own thoughts and feelings included since apparently I had started to confuse myself.

One eye popped open when I felt a bottle pressed into my hand. I glanced down at the ale before looking up to find Angel and gave her a weak smile. She knew something was up with me, she had known me almost my entire life. She had picked up on the subtle changes in my demeanor the last couple weeks. I wasn't ready to tell her more about it than I already had, more because I didn't want to admit it to myself, maybe I would get there eventually. Yeah, and maybe pigs would sprout wings and fly. I tipped the neck of the bottle her direction in thanks then raised it to my lips. I took a long drink as she settled in beside me.

"So how's it feel to have Saturday off again?"

I chuckled, knowing full well there were other things she wanted to talk to me about. Being who she was she wouldn't push. She would wait patiently while I figured my shit out and let me come to her with it. I appreciated that about my best friend and I wished I was the type of person who could express it to her properly but emotional displays were never my thing. She got that too.

"It feels amazing. I hated that project, they can update and firewall their own damn systems next time."

She laughed, knowing better than to think I would ever turn down the overtime when it was offered, even if it did dampen my weekends.

"Sure they can. So, anything planned for tonight now that you're free of the wired cage?"

I turned my head to look at her. She wanted to know if I planned on going out tonight. I shrugged and glanced at the small charcoal grill and picnic table we'd set up in the park. James was involved in an intense conversation with Courtney, who had actually bothered to show up but had yet to speak to me. The look on her face was easy as hell to read and I actually wondered, if I managed to see it, how James missed it.

Courtney was hanging on her every word, wide eyed and smiling. She looked completely in love. I was a total asshole and I knew it, but I hadn't known as much at the time. Back when I had recruited James as my project and turned her into a mini-me. I let out a heavy sigh and turned my attention back to Angel, feigning a happy smile as best I could.

"I dunno. Maybe. All feels so... I don't even know...Silly I guess."

I drained the beer in my hand, levered myself out of the chair, tossed the bottle and grabbed another before returning to my seat.

"Silly, huh? How so?"

She had one eyebrow raised at me, daring me to be totally honest with her and for a moment I really wanted to be.

"I don't know what I mean, Angel. Maybe nothing. Maybe I'm just tired, too much overtime."

I chuckled nervously and caught her rolling her eyes at me in my peripheral vision, she knew better but wasn't about to push.

"Good to see Court here, huh?"

"Yeah, it is. I just wish she would actually speak to me. I mean, it's not like I screwed her over intentionally. I had no idea how she felt about James." I caught Angel's look out of the corner of my eye and turned my gaze on her fully. "What?"

"Are you serious right now?"

"Of course I am."

"You're telling me that if you'd known that Courtney had a thing for James you wouldn't have brought her over to the dark side and taught her all your seedy ways? Really?"

Despite the teasing look on her face her words irritated me. I was sure it showed right across my face because Zara made her way over to where we were settled in to interject if things got nasty.

"What kind of prick do you think I am, Angel? You've known me longer than anyone..."

"Everything okay guys?"

Zara's voice broke through my agitated tone but I tossed a hand up to shush her so I could finish what I was saying.

"I may not be the relationship type, hell, I may be heading toward being a total emotional black hole but that doesn't mean I expect everyone to be. Jesus, you really think that the world would be better with more people like me in it? 'Cause frankly, I don't. Thanks for the vote of confidence though *bestie*. Glad to know you think so damn highly of me."

I dropped my recently replaced, and still full, beer bottle on the ground next to my chair, shoved out of it and started to walk off. The feel of a hand on my wrist stopped me and made me turn around, a glare leveled on my best friend as she stood to meet me at eye level.

"Come on, Lux. You know that's not what I meant... Don't get all pissed off at me just because you can't work out your emotional shit."

"Fuck you."

I yanked my wrist from her grip, spun on my heel and started toward my car. I needed to get away from whatever the hell had decided to happen right then.

"Lux! Come back!"

I ignored the pleading in Angel's voice. I knew my outburst had grabbed the attention of the three friends who hadn't been standing right there next to us. I didn't care, I was pissed and only about half of the rage I was feeling was toward Angel. I was mad at myself for things I couldn't admit, not even in my head.

"Hey Lux."

The familiar voice to my right pulled me up short and shot my heart right into my throat. My stomach knotted up hard as I turned to face the person creating all the havoc in my life. Rascal stood there, a smile on her face and her arm around some girl.

"This is Kayla. Babe, this is my friend Lux."

My breath caught a little as I gave the new girl a once over. She was cute, which I hated to admit. About Rascal's height with honey blonde hair, pale blue eyes and a figure which would have knocked me right on my ass had she not been snuggled in close to Rascal. My eyes flickered to my friends hand on the girls' hip and narrowed. My breath caught as I shook my head and turned toward my car.

"Okay, nice to meet you too. Rude much?"

I bit my tongue to keep from turning my still smoldering temper on Kayla, she was playing with fire and didn't even know it. I needed to get out of there, get away from it all and as sad as it sounded, I knew exactly how to chase away what was happening in my head. I slipped into my car, started it and tore away from the curb, intent on leaving the things I'd been feeling behind in the park. I disregarded the speed limit all the way back out to San Tan Valley and pulled into the driveway at the house much faster than I should have.

Thankfully the local police had apparently been otherwise engaged and I hadn't been pulled over but I should really learn to be more careful when driving angry. I slammed into the house then into my bedroom, changed my clothes and glanced at the clock on my bedside table. It was a little early to make my usual bar and club rounds but today I didn't really care. I was in a mood and needed a few drinks. I popped open the recently installed Uber app on my phone, ordered a ride and then made sure I had my wallet and keys.

The ride into Scottsdale was a bit of a hike from the house I lived in and my driver attempted to be social. I wasn't feeling up to talking. I answered a couple questions but overall sat in the back of the car in silence watching the buildings zip past. I left the driver a tip before exiting the vehicle and I made my way toward the nearest dining establishment. I had decided on the drive I needed to eat something before I went to drown my sorrows in a bottle of rum. I picked a place, was seated and ordered my food, staring at the table as I waited for it to arrive.

I ate silently and tried not to think about anything other than why I was out, what I was attempting tonight. I felt numb, hollow and I didn't know if my usual habit of drinking too much and falling into bed with some strange woman would help. I was damn sure going to try. I finished as much of my food as I could, not really as hungry as I should have been since I was still fuming. I paid my bill, dropped a few dollars on the table and then made my way out onto the sidewalk to decide where I was going.

I ended up wandering the streets of Scottsdale for at least three hours, not my finest evening but I was so lost in every way I could be. I finally stopped and took a deep breath then did a double check of where the hell I was. I found that while my thoughts and emotions might be a lost, tangled mess at least I knew where I was physically. I started walking again, making a few well-known turns here and there and finally landing where I wanted to be. I stepped into the bar, still earlier than I would usually be but not feeling as awkward about it as I would have earlier in the day.

I weaved my way to the bar, ordered a Captain and coke and then made my way to a table in the corner to watch people filter in. It wouldn't take too long for the place to fill up and I needed the heated, sweaty press of too many bodies right then. I took a deep breath, exhaled heavily and downed half my drink as the early crowd filtered into the space. It should be a good night and I was hoping for plenty of beautiful ladies to choose from. I didn't even care if they were with someone or not tonight.

I knocked back the rest of my drink and returned to the bar for another, downing it before I even bothered to move and ordering a third. I was looking to push my limits tonight, to see what would happen. I was a bit curious how drunk I could really get and if it would even help. If my best friend thought I was such a lost cause then I was really screwed. In that case there really wasn't any point in trying to fight it any longer. I was what I was and apparently it wasn't going to change. I was a terrible person who didn't give a shit about anyone but myself.

Two people I thought loved me as I was had told me exactly as much in the last couple weeks so it must be true. If that was the case, I'd start making sure I acted it and was a terrible as they seemed to think I was. I started scanning the room, taking my third drink slower than the first two. I needed to at least be able to speak if I was leaving with someone after all. I was taking my time tonight, I needed something different, someone different, not that it wasn't a different someone every time I did this but I tended to have a type. It was high time I broke out of the pathetic round of not so subtle choices in women and think outside the box a little bit.

I was on my fourth drink when I spotted her, my prey for the night. I couldn't help the slight twitch at the left corner of my mouth as I watched her dance. She was surrounded by people on the dancefloor, male and female. She didn't seem to actually be dancing with any of them exclusively though. I finished my drink and pushed away from the table as I discarded the empty glass on top of it. I took a breath and started through the crowd toward her. She was taller than me, but she had on some serious heels so if I had to guess she was actually closer to my height without them.

A sweep of pale blonde hair graced the tops of her shoulders. A quick look at her eyebrows told me the color was natural and she was gorgeous. I paused at the edge of the dancefloor. Her hair was cut and styled just so and brushing the tops of her shoulders as she moved. I couldn't tell what color her eyes were. Not that I really gave a damn. She looked to be in her early twenties, maybe twenty-two or so and had some fruity looking pink drink in her hand, half gone.

I raked my eyes down her body as she danced, enjoying every move she made. The task was easy since she had chosen to wear a skirt which would make more sense as a belt and a tank top I could almost see through. I wasn't complaining and from the look of it neither were any of the guys dancing around her. I smirked as she turned a little in her movement, giving me a nice view of her perfectly-shaped ass. Oh yeah, this one was mine. All I had to do was go seal the deal and my night was set.

I stepped onto the dancefloor and made my way through the rapidly expanding crowd to the woman, my focus on her the entire time. I slipped up close and stepped in behind her not hesitating for even a moment before my hands found her hips. She started, the little jump making her muscles twitch. She recovered quickly and glanced over her shoulder to see who had touched her. I admit she shocked me by raising an eyebrow and then leaning back into me. Well, they usually took a little more work, but I wasn't complaining, not tonight.

A few of the men who had been dancing around her stopped dead and watched us, mouths hanging open and eyes wide. It was the beginning of every straight man's wet dream and I was fine playing it up for them some. I slipped my arms boldly around the slim waist my hands had been resting on. The smirk I'd been wearing grew into a cocky smile when I felt the woman in my arms shift. She reached up and slid a hand onto the back of my neck.

This one was bold and I was going to take full advantage of it as quickly as I possibly could.

I pulled her back tight against me, our bodies melding together as our hips moved through a sexy little bump and grind. The alcohol was already going to my head and I was feeling fearless. I also felt sexy which was helped by the fact I caught as many eyes on me as were on her. I knew while I wasn't as feminine as this woman, I wasn't bad to look at and that was apparent tonight. I felt a slap on my ass but only rolled my eyes and kept dancing.

The song changed and the sexy blonde decided she wanted a change of position. She turned in my arms, wrapped her own arms around my neck and pulled her right knee up to my hip. I grabbed hold of her thigh with my left hand. My right hand found its way onto her back and under the almost pointless tank top. She shocked me yet again by leaning in closer and ghosting her lips along my jawline. I definitely hadn't seen the move coming but who was I to try and stop her? I waited for her to make it along my jaw to my chin and then decided to make a bold move of my own.

I shifted enough for my lips to meet hers. I felt her take a sharp breath in surprise, but then she stunned me again by leaning into me and kissing me back. A few cheers went up from the guys dancing around us then faded out as I flicked my tongue along her lips and she opened to me without hesitation. The kiss deepened, going on for several minutes before we pulled back. We were both breathing heavily and I caught her smiling at me. I leaned in, brushing my lips across her cheek to her ear, shivered when I felt her tongue on my ear lobe and then gathered myself enough to speak.

"Wanna get out of here?"

"Bathroom... Now."

The jump in my pulse at her two very steady and commanding words was a little ridiculous but I nodded and eased my grip on her. Her leg dropped and she led the way across the room. A few of the guys pouted, booed and made dirty remarks as we worked through the flood of people. We both made a point of ignoring them. She pushed open the door to the bathroom and practically dragged me to the largest stall on the end. She slammed the door closed before locking it.

As soon as it latched I grabbed her arm, spun her around and backed her against the wall, pinning her between the cold, blue tile and my body. My lips found her neck and she let out something between a sigh and a moan at the contact. The sound fueled the fire raging through my body. I yanked her short skirt up around her hips finding barely-there panties. I wasted very little time pushing my hand down the front of the sheer, lacey fabric of her thong.

The bathroom door opened as the tip of my finger found her clit. She either hadn't heard it or didn't care since she let out a loud moan at the contact. There were few things in the world sexier to me than a woman who wasn't ashamed to be vocal. The noise caused my breath to catch in my throat. I circled her clit a few times then dipped my hand lower, my fingers slipping between her lips and into the wetness waiting there. She was as ready as I was, good thing since I wasn't in the mood for slow and teasing.

I ran my fingers around her opening a couple times but then heard her whimper and whisper, "Fuck me" in my ear and I came undone. I pushed two fingers into her as deep as I could. I was not being gentle. She cried out as her nails dug into my shoulders through my own tank top. Her head fell back against the wall as I bit my lower lip. I used my free left hand to pull her right knee up to my hip like it had been in the dancefloor as I slid my fingers out then thrust them back in hard. Her hands found their way under my tank, her nails biting into my skin as I pressed my hips closer, using my body as pressure on the back of my wrist, forcing my fingers deeper into her as roughly as I could.

The sounds she was letting out into my ear made my eyes flutter closed while my fingers dug into her thigh. My lips connected with her neck again and I only hesitated a moment before I bit down. I had chosen the soft skin at the base of her neck, drawing it into my mouth and sucking hard. She whimpered in response and I grinned as I marked her. She hadn't even asked my name but she would sure as hell remember me tomorrow. I curled the tips of my fingers as I thrust into her which dragged another loud moan from her as my lips disconnected from her neck.

I had to lean my head back slightly so could breathe a little better. The mark was already beginning to darken around hints of teeth marks and I grinned. I closed my eyes and tilted my hand so the heel of my hand pressed into her clit. I winced and let out a soft growl as her nails broke the skin on my shoulders. I didn't even consider stopping though, not now, not when I could feel how close she was.

A few flicks of my fingertips later and she crashed over the edge into her orgasm, hard. She dragged her nails down my back roughly as she screamed into the tiled room. The sound echoed as she tightened around my fingers and I let my grin become a wicked smile as I slowed my movements. I helped her ride the wave as long as she could, making it last. When she finally started to relax I eased my fingers from inside her and released her leg so her foot could settle onto the floor again.

I stayed pressed close against her until I thought she could support her own weight and then took half a step back and smiled at her. Her eyes fluttered open and she gave me a smile back, easy and definitely satisfied which always made me feel better.

"Damn. I admit, I wasn't quite expecting *that* when I agreed to come out with my friends tonight."

I chuckled and offered her a quick shrug in response. Very few of the women I picked up expected it to happen when they left their houses. She seemed to focus on something then, one brow arcing up perfectly.

"What's your name anyway?"

"Lux."

"Lux, I like it. I'm Megan."

Even though it felt somewhat silly to do so after what had happened less than two minutes earlier, I offered her my hand, which she took.

"Nice to meet you, Megan."

We both laughed at the sheer weirdness of what we had done and then I shook my head and cleared my throat.

"Well, this was fun but, I gotta run."

She dropped my hand and raised that eyebrow at me again. She tugged her skirt back into place which made me pause for a moment.

"Don't run off yet, we aren't nearly finished."

I glanced down as she grabbed my wrist. My gaze moved back up, a smirk on my lips, as she tugged me over. She turned and pinned me against the wall space she had just vacated. While I never expected such things to happen, it was always nice when they did. I wasn't in any position to argue with her. She pressed my shoulders back against the wall. I took in a sharp breath through clenched teeth as my broken skin pressed into the fabric of my tank top. I was pretty sure I was bleeding, maybe I could return the favor in the next few minutes.

I let myself be pinned to the tile, still warmed by Megan's body heat and I felt myself flush in response. She wasted no time, as eager to get to it as I had been which was fine since I was more than ready to go. She popped the button on my jeans, dragged the zipper down and then yanked them down off my hips and to the floor in one pull. Well damn.

She leaned in before I could comment, catching my off guard with the sudden movement. Her tongue met the wetness which had been building between my legs for the last several minutes. It only took seconds for me to realize she knew exactly what she was doing. I closed my eyes and leaned my head back against the wall, glad to not be instructing this time. The tip of her tongue darted out and flicked across my clit causing my muscles to twitch as a moan slipped past my lips. I wasn't about to be any quieter than she had been. I didn't give a shit who heard me getting off, I liked an audience.

I reached down and slipped my fingers through her hair, the golden strands softer than they had looked. My gaze drifted down so I could watch her on her knees in front of me and oh how I loved the sight. My breathing hitched as she traced a finger through my slick heat, but I kept my eyes on her. I twisted some of her hair around my fingers and gave a light, experimental pull to which she gasped and dug her fingers into my hip. Oh, I liked this one.

I let her play for a few more seconds since she was doing an amazing job. My pulse was increasing rapidly and my breathing had become more ragged with each flick of her tongue. I finally gave her hair a hard yank, pulling her away from what she was doing and dragging her up to my lips. I kissed her hard, tasting myself. Her hand went to work in place of her mouth without missing a beat. My hips picked up a rhythm against her hand all on their own.

Her tongue danced with mine as she worked her hand lower. I had less than a second of advance warning before I felt two fingers push inside me. I broke away from her lips with a harsh growl and brought my free hand to her bare shoulder. My short nails dug into bare skin as hers had done to me a short time earlier. I fully expected us to be interrupted at any moment but I wasn't about to leave the stall until I was done. She seemed intent on the same goal and the pace of her thrusts told me as much.

"Harder."

The word barely made it past my lips and I hardly recognized the voice as my own. She caught the word when it brushed against her own lips however. She willingly obliged my request. The sudden intensity was exactly what I wanted, and needed. Somehow I was still caught off guard and I leaned my head against her shoulder as a couple choice expletives fell from my mouth. My short cropped nails dragged hard down her shoulder, no doubt taking skin with them. She honestly didn't seem to mind so I didn't try to stop.

She did what I had done and leaned her body close. Using her hip as leverage against the back of her hand she drove her fingers as deep as they could go. I was so turned on with the thought of being overheard, being caught it didn't take long to push me into my climax. I actually screamed out her name. I shivered as my muscles began to relax and felt her step away from me, freeing her fingers from inside me. I melted back against the tiled wall until my legs were working properly and then shook myself. I pulled my pants up, buttoned them and gave her a smile.

"Well, that was, something else. Damn."

All she did in response was grin and wink at me before she unlocked the stall, stepped out and moved to the mirror to check herself. She was fixing her hair by the time I exited the stall and moved toward the large mirror to do the same. Thankfully my short hair was easy to tame back into place. I cast a glance over to the woman on my left as she got her gold locks under control with a smirk. I had always loved that 'just been fucked' look, even more when I was the cause of it. It was so damn sexy.

"Thanks for the romp, Megan. Have a great night."

She grinned and shot me another wink before I turned and exited the bathroom. I was glad she didn't seem intent on following me or getting weird about what had happened. I felt better by the barest degree and wondered for a moment if I should try for a double. After a moment to think on it, during which time I rolled my shoulders and winced again, I decided against it.

I made my way to the bar and loaded up my app again, checking how far away the nearest drivers happened to be, noticing a few fairly close. I decided against another drink and ordered the ride as I made my way toward the front door of the place. I had enough time to get in a smoke before my ride showed up. I pulled out the pack as soon as I hit the door and tapped one out, brought it to my lips then lit it. It was an early night all things considered but I had done what I had come out to do.

My mind was blissfully clear and I didn't know if it was thanks to the alcohol or Megan. I really didn't even care anymore. I smoked in silence, a small grin on my face as I waited on my ride which pulled up just as I finished exhaling my last drag and flicked the butt into the street. What timing. I climbed into the car and settled in for the ride back to the house. I did my best to stay awake, not wanting to doze off on the poor driver and leave the guy having to wake me up when we made it.

A while later I spilled myself out of the backseat of the Mazda that had transported me. I dropped a few dollars on his front seat as a tip and shuffled up to the front door. It was early for me but I felt like death and I was ready to take a shower and crawl into bed. After working for the last eight or nine Saturdays I wasn't used to the weekend activity anymore. My job entailed a lot of sitting on the floor and connecting wires then sitting at desks and connecting networks.

I yawned as I stepped into the house, shut the door and made my way toward the living room. I stopped short when I heard my roommates talking in the kitchen. I wasn't in the mood to deal with any of them after the botched afternoon. I hadn't really considered it before coming home so early. I muttered a few curses under my breath and then took a deep breath then went to deal with them. I had heard Angel and James at the very least.

"Hey Lux! What's up?"

Apparently no one had told James exactly what had gone down at the park earlier since she seemed as friendly and perky as ever. I knew she had heard me when I raised my voice but I wasn't sure if she had heard what I'd said or if anyone had filled her in on the whole ordeal. I gave her a small nod and a half-assed noncommittal noise and then turned toward the hallway that led to my bedroom.

"Really? Just gonna ignore me?"

Angel's voice stopped me and I stood stock still for a moment before I turned around and leveled a death glare at her.

"Would you rather I yell at you again? Because right now, it's yell at you or ignore you."

I had managed to make it through the words without shouting but it was strained and my jaw was tense. The rest of my body had followed suit.

"No I'd rather we be adults about this and actually talk."

I let the glare stay on her for a few seconds while I thought about it, not really sure that I wanted to talk to her. She'd hurt me, pissed me off to more accurate. I wanted to be alone, or at the very least away from her. The sound of someone clearing their throat to my left caught my attention and when I jerked my head around the deep, chocolate brown eyes mine settled on softened my expression noticeably.

"Hey Rascal."

She gave me a small smile and I attempted to give her one back. All I could see in my mind was her with the girl at the park, her arm around her waist. My expression fell from angry to hurt and I turned away before she could see it. I headed toward my room again, not stopping this time. I stepped in and all but slammed the door, wanting it all to fade away and leave me alone. I had been in such a good mood before I stepped into the house. Somehow the assessment didn't seem quite right but I took a death grip on it anyway.

My roommates continued talking in the kitchen and living room. I didn't care enough to try and listen. I kicked off my shoes and fell on top of my bed, not bothering with pulling back the blanket or changing out of my clothes. I laid there and stared at the wall, willing the hurt away. Of course, it didn't go away because I was avoiding the one thing which would make it go away. If anything, laying there listening to the laughter coming from the other side of my door made it worse.

I was aching inside but I was too proud, and too set in my ways, to admit why. Even if it was in the dark of my room and only to myself. Admitting it made it real, made it a thing I had to deal with and I didn't want to deal with it. I didn't want to have to deal with my feelings. Feelings I never wanted to have and were only getting stronger the more I attempted to ignore them. I turned onto my side, curled into myself and cried for the first time in longer than I could really remember.

I hurt and I hated it. I wanted the waves of emotions I was feeling to go away, to leave me alone and let me have my life back. If only someone had bothered to tell me when you start falling for someone, it rarely goes away. Ignoring it doesn't help at all. Not that I could have helped it, I hadn't even seen it coming, it had blindsided me and I wasn't ready to deal with it.

Chapter Six

Friday, March 20th, 2009 – San Tan Valley, Arizona

I spent the week avoiding my roommates at all costs. Actually, I spent it ignoring all my friends, which was starting to suck. I was feeling particularly melancholy and didn't know what to do about it. The only solution was the usual one, talking to the very people I was trying to stay clear of. I sat in the driveway, the engine cut off but not willing to leave the front seat and go inside. If the car sitting in our driveway and the others on the street were any indication we had a full house.

Angel, James, Rascal, Zara, Dani and, from the looks of the car I didn't recognize, probably Rascal's new girlfriend. I didn't have it in me to face them, but I wasn't in any condition to go out and get up to my usual tricks either. My mind was a terrible swirling mass of indecision which had left me sitting in my front seat. I picked at my steering wheel cover and tried to decide what to do, going to Zara and Dani's was out since they were obviously inside.

I finally gave up with a low grumble and shoved my door open, slipped from the vehicle, and made my way to the front door. Now that I was out in the air rather than cooped up in a closed off space I could hear the entire group out in the backyard and smell the grill. Maybe, just maybe, I was lucky enough to slip in without being noticed and could sneak into my room and be left alone for the night. I eased the front door open and stepped inside, glad it sounded like everyone was outside. I started toward the living room which would leave me with a short skip to my bedroom and safety.

"Hey Lux!"

Damn. No such luck, I should have known better. My luck with anything outside of picking up beautiful women was terrible.

"Hey Dani."

I turned toward my friend and did my best impression of a smile for her sake. I knew any one of my friends would see right through it but at least I tried.

"What's up? You've been avoiding us all week."

"No I haven't."

She stopped me by putting a hand up then walked over and gave me a rather rough punch in the arm, it made me wince.

"Ow! Hey!"

"Don't you lie to me, Lux. We all know you better than that. After that blow out with Angel last week you've been steering clear of all of us. What's going on?"

I shook my head as I glanced out the back sliding glass door. My gaze found Rascal, her arm settled around the cute blonde girl from the park, what had her name been? Kayla. My brows knit together and my eyes misted over as a frown settled on my features making Dani follow my gaze.

"Oh, shit, I get it now."

"Get what? There's nothing to fucking *get* Dani. Just leave it alone, okay?"

"Lux, quit it. You're obviously fighting it and lashing out at the rest of us because of it."

"Because of what?"

I shouted the words at her, not caring if anyone else heard me. I was mentally exhausted and I didn't want to think about anything she was saying. She grabbed my arm and dragged me down the hall, into my bedroom and swung the door closed behind us. It didn't latch but it did shut us off from everyone else.

"Look, Lux, you really need to get your shit together and figure this out. You have feelings for her, it's pretty fucking obvious. Deal with that, however you need to, but deal with it. I'm a little tired of dealing with your bullshit because of it."

The door eased open and Zara poked her head into the room. She must have gone looking for Dani and heard her chewing me out in the bedroom.

"Dani, what's going on? You okay Lux? You look... Irritated."

"I *am* irritated thanks to your girlfriend. Get her out of my face before I knock her on her ass."

Zara shot me a look I'd never seen cross her face before and I had the distinct impression I had crossed the line.

"Let it be Zara, she's just pissed at me because I called her out on her feelings and she hates it."

The look which passed between the two told me Zara understood what she was talking about. My anger rocketed to a whole new level.

"Why the hell is everyone in my business? Huh? I mean, really guys, how I may or may not feel about anyone is *my* business, not yours, not Angel's, not Court's, so just lay the hell off, okay?"

Dani looked like she was about to say something in response to my outburst but Zara stopped her.

"Calm down, both of you. Jesus, you are the two *worst* people to have arguing about anything. Both so damn stubborn. Dani, get back to the party and give me a few minutes with Lux, please?"

Dani huffed at her girlfriend but then nodded and left my bedroom to go back to everyone leaving me alone with Zara.

"Look, Lux, she's a spitfire and gets a little too heated sometimes but, Dani isn't wrong sweetie. It's pretty obvious there's something there and it's eating at you. Wanna talk about it?"

My eyes found my boots as I dropped onto my bed, sitting on the edge, elbows on my knees and head hanging. I was such a jerk and I had no excuse for it, all my friends had been trying to do was help me and I'd been lashing out at them.

"What happened with Angel at the park? You know she wasn't trying to come down on you, she was asking a legitimate question. We've all wondered exactly what she asked you at some point or another, Lux, she was just the only one that said it. We've been worried about it pissing you off so we kept quiet."

"I'm a jerk."

"A little bit, but you know what? We love you anyway."

"I know you do, all of you. I know I've been terrible lately I'm just so..."

"Confused?"

I nodded, it was all I could give her for a response because I was starting to get emotional and it was spiking my irritation again.

"Lux, this thing you have about Rebecca, how long has it been going on?"

I shook my head and turned away from her. I didn't want to talk about it, didn't want to give it a timeline, or a voice. It would make it too real. It couldn't be real, I wasn't ready for it.

"Okay, you don't have to talk about it right now but, honey, you need to talk about it with someone, eventually. If you don't it will eat away at you. You're already pushing us away. As much as we love you, how much more do you think we'll take before we stop trying to push back?"

Her words sank their way into me, hitting my very soul and making me panic. The thought of my friends ever not being there not something I was ready to accept.

"Zara, is it that bad? Am *I* that bad?"

"Not yet, sweetie, but you're getting there. Fast. Figure it out, deal with it, decide what the hell you want and make it work. Just stop lashing out at us. Please."

I gave her another nod as I dropped my face into my hands. I let out a heavy sigh as I fought back the rush of emotions trying to fly to the surface.

"Zara?"

"Hmmm?"

"Can you send Angel in here? Please?"

She offered me a small smile and nodded before she left my bedroom silently. Hopefully she was headed out to send Angel back to talk to me. I had to hope I hadn't pushed hard enough to make my best friend want nothing to do with me. I was terrified of losing her.

"What?"

The voice made me look up and give my best friend a soft, sheepish smile where she stood holding my doorknob but not actually standing in my room.

"Can you come in and sit down?"

"Why?"

God she still sounded pissed. I didn't blame her, I had really screwed up this time and I had to try and fix it.

"Because I need to apologize to you and I wanna do it properly. Please?"

She huffed at me then slipped into my room, closed the door and settled herself on the side of the bed next to me. I turned so I was facing her and tried to get my rampaging mind under control.

"Angel, I was out of line last week. I know you had every right to ask me what you did. I mean, I haven't exactly been a shining example of monogamy or anything so, it makes sense everyone would think I don't care about *any* relationships. It's not true though. I would never try to get between Zara and Danielle and I never would have gotten Jamie involved in my lifestyle if I'd known how Courtney felt about her."

Her focus narrowed in on me further at the use of our friends' actual names rather than their nicknames. For a few long seconds she seemed to be studying me, looking for the truth in my words.

"You really mean that don't you?"

"Of course I do. Look, I know I'm hopeless, okay? I'm beyond saving and so far past being able to be with someone that it's not funny. But that doesn't mean I don't want you guys to be happy. All of you."

"Even Rascal?"

Ouch. She couldn't help herself could she? She had to bring it up again when it was the last thing I wanted to talk about, ever.

"Angel, I honestly don't know what you want me say to that. Why wouldn't I want her happy too?"

"I think you do want her happy, just maybe, not with Kayla?"

"Why would I have a problem with Kayla? I don't even know her?"

The words even sounded weak to my own ears. Like I didn't really mean them despite how true they might actually be.

"Oh honey. That might work with anyone *other* than me. I know you, Lux, remember? I know this look you have, this moody, brooding, pissy little tantrum you've been throwing the last few weeks. It's really unattractive and it's not doing anyone any good, including you."

I hated it when she was right. It made me want to push her off of something, but instead I sighed and looked over at her again.

"Damn you. I wish you would stop that."

"Never, I care too damn much about you to let you wallow in self-pity and misery. Now come on, talk woman."

"I don't know what to do, Angel. I'm so lost, I've never felt like this before and it's driving me completely batty."

"You care about her?"

"She's one of my best friends, of course I care about her."

She gave me the look. The one eyebrow arced, lips curled slightly look which says "You know that's not what I meant." We all have a friend who has the look, Angel had perfected it with me over the last several years. She was pulling out all the stops with it now.

"Jesus, fine, I... Kinda, maybe, have feelings for her, okay?"

"Feelings? Really? That's the best you can do? You have *feelings* for her. Christ Lux, you're almost thirty, grow a pair!"

"Oh my g... Fine, fine. I, I'm..."

I was trying, I really was, but it was hard for me. I couldn't remember ever uttering the words trying to find themselves leaving my mouth and it was awkward.

"I love her."

Saying it did exactly what I thought it would. The wall which had been slowly cracking over the last few weeks came crashing down around me. Everything I had been trying desperately to tamp down, to conceal and to completely ignore surfaced in a wall slamming into me and took my breath away. I sat there, stunned I had let those words fall from my mouth and then it happened, the tears started. I hated crying, it felt so awkward and unnatural to me since I did it so infrequently. There I sat all the same, tears streaking silently down my face.

"Come here."

Angel said the words but didn't actually give me any choice in the matter. She slid over and wrapped her arms around me. I thought about pulling away, about sticking with my usual defense to crying and shutting her out to deal with it on my own. Something about the usual approach felt wrong though and this time I didn't want to deal with it alone. I didn't think I could. It took all of three seconds for me to lean into my best friend and bury my face in her shoulder.

"It'll be okay, Lux."

"No Angel, it won't. It can't be okay."

I sniffed before I leaned away from the soaked patch I had made on her shirt and shook my head at the look on her face.

"Why not? Give me one good reason that it can't be okay?"

"There's no way it can ever work."

"And why is that?"

"She's better off where she is, Angel. With Kayla. I'm no good for her, she deserves better."

My eyebrows knit together at the chuckle she let out when she shook her head at me and I wondered what could possibly be funny.

"Lux, that's exactly why it could work. You've been a little bit, ummm, out there, but you know that. You admit it and you care enough about her to think she deserves better. What she deserves is to know how you feel about her."

"God, Angel. I can't tell her, definitely not while she's... She's still with Kayla."

It was so hard to even say her name knowing she was out there, right at that moment, all over the girl I had finally confessed to loving. My life was a mess and I had no one to blame for it but myself. I was starting up a fairly good job of doing exactly that, blaming myself.

"Stop it. You know how she is, Lux. It'll last a few more weeks and then she'll dump her and be over it. They never last."

She was right, they didn't and it made me begin to wonder why. She always seemed so intense with them in the beginning.

"Why don't they last, Angel? And what if I wait it out, Kayla leaves, I tell her how I feel and then I only last a couple months? Then what?"

It was a valid question and from the look she was giving me she agreed. She also had a response to it.

"Look, I haven't actually chatted with her about this so, I'm just guessing but... Lux, I think they don't last because they aren't you."

The words made my head snap up and my eyes find hers to make sure she wasn't screwing with me. She looked completely serious.

"What?"

"Like I said, I don't know for sure. We've all been terrified to bring this up with either of you but, girl, the way she looks at you when she thinks no one is watching. I think she's been in love with you for a while."

I was in shock and I wanted to know if she was right. If she was, I'd never seen any proof of it. I almost didn't dare hope she was right because if I got my hopes up and she'd been wrong it might crush me.

"Talk to her. Seriously. I can send her in here if you want..."

"No. I can't do that to her. She needs to see this through with Kayla, see where it goes on her own terms. I can't get between them."

Angel smiled at me and shook her head as she leaned over and kissed me on the forehead lightly.

"After that I'd better not *ever* hear you say she deserves better than you again. Hear me?"

I let out a soft laugh and nodded, getting where she was coming from even if I still wasn't sure it was true. She gave me one last hug and then exited my room, leaving me alone with my thoughts and the emotions. I had opened up and admitted my feelings and they were definitely happy to be free. I considered going out and joining everyone but then changed my mind.

I wouldn't split Rascal and Kayla up, but I wasn't exactly ready to share space with the two of them being cute together either. I stretched out on my bed, propped my arms behind my head and sighed at the ceiling. I hoped for some easy answers to find me. I knew they wouldn't come or if answers did find me, they wouldn't be easy, but I could dream. After a while I decided I needed to do something other than sit in my room so I pushed up off the mattress and readied myself to enter the fray.

It turned out my trepidation was unwarranted since I exited my bedroom into an empty house. I had no clue where everyone had gone or even when they had left. I had apparently been lost in thought longer than I realized, and deeper as well since I hadn't even heard them leave. It was fine though, I could use some time alone and didn't want to have to actually leave the house, only my room. I plopped myself down on the couch and flipped on the massive television. I loaded up Netflix after the newest update installed.

I scanned through the recommended titles and made a face, wondering who had been rating things on my account. It had to be Angel, everything it wanted me to watch was some kind of cheesy chick flick and I had never been into those. I double checked the thing, making sure it was signed into my profile. It was so I decided I needed to have a chat with Angel about using the one I had created for her.

I grumbled at the screen and then flipped over to search, tapped in a few letters and selected the first season of Criminal Minds. I had seen them all but it was something I enjoyed enough to watch again and could zone out in the middle of and not miss anything. I leaned back, settling into the comfort of the couch and let the sound of the show fade into the background. My mind wandered as the familiar voices filled the room. I had to try and get a grip on the emotions rampaging through me.

It wouldn't do me any good to get weepy and hurt every time I had to see Rascal with the blonde knockout. The most obvious solution would be to just avoid them at all costs. Though it might cause some questions among the entire group. It was time to decide if I had it in me to be the actress I'd never attempted to become. I wasn't about to move, I loved the house and the neighborhood. Plus the low rent was allowing me to save enough money to be fine whenever I decided to retire.

I didn't have it in me to cut all contact with Rascal, even the thought of it made my chest tighten up. I had to think of something else to ease the sudden pain. The reaction decided for me, it was strong enough to make me realize having to watch her be with someone else was better than not seeing her at all. I would plaster on a fake smile and pretend seeing her with Kayla wasn't killing me inside.

I started awake some time later, Criminal Minds still playing on the TV and voices drawing me back into consciousness. I rubbed my eyes to force them into focus and then exhaled sharply as I sat up and settled my feet back on the floor. Laughter drew my gaze toward the hallway leading in from the entry. I managed a grin as Angel and James came through into the kitchen. The smile faltered slightly when Rascal and her new girlfriend walked in behind them. I managed to recover and force the smile back into place before they saw it.

One glance at Angel told me she had seen the slip and she offered me a small smile before she turned back to whatever James was saying to her. I did my best to feign interest in the episode playing on the TV but I couldn't block out the sound of Rascal laughing. My eyes kept trying to slide over to the loveseat she and Kayla had settled onto but I forced my vision to stay focused ahead. I could catch glimpses of them out of the corner of my eye though and seeing Rascal sitting on her lap, cuddled in close and playing with her hair was almost too much.

I did what I could to ignore them. To block out the giggles and the cute little comments passing between them. It was taking every bit of self-control I had to bite my tongue and let it happen. The muscles in my jaw were working overtime as I fought the urge to open my mouth and I knew they would be sore later. I was rapidly reaching the end of my rope and knew I wasn't going to be able to keep quiet much longer. This endeavor was proving to be a lot harder than I had expected it to be.

"Hey Kayla?"

Angel had spoken up but I wasn't sure what she planned to say to this woman who was wholly unwelcome in my space.

"Yeah?"

"Didn't you say you have an early shift at work tomorrow?"

"Yep, early start on Saturdays. Go in at around seven."

"Well it's getting late, maybe you should head out soon."

I saw Kayla check her watch out of the corner of my eye and then heard her let out a sigh. She nodded, slid Rascal off her lap and then stood with her and nodded toward the door.

"Had fun today, see you guys later."

She tossed a wave at my friends and they gave her nods in response before the pair left the living room and headed back out to Kayla's car. Once they were out the front door, James headed up to her room to change and Angel joined me on the couch.

"That looked like it was hard on you."

I nodded, unable to speak until the muscles relaxed and my jaw started working again.

"Are you sure you want to just let this run its course? This thing with Kayla?"

"It's not a matter of what I want Angel, it's a matter of what has to happen. If that relationship is going to end, it needs to end because of those two, not because of me."

"I know you keep saying that but, do you have it in you to sit back and watch them together until that eventually happens?"

"I wish I knew. That was... It sucked so bad."

"I know it did. It probably won't get any easier though, you know that right?"

I did know, it was only going to get worse and my heart sank as my stomach knotted up at the thought.

"I don't know how much I can take, but I'm sure as hell going to stomach as much of it as I can before I need to distance myself."

I heard a sigh from beside me and caught my best friends nod. Her head fell onto my shoulder as the front door opened and then closed again. Rascal walked back into the room and started chatting with Angel, I tuned it all out. I wasn't sure I could handle the pep in her voice given the reason for it. I heard the microwave and the muffled sound of popcorn popping and kept my eyes forward, staring at the TV, not catching the conversation.

"Alright, I'm heading to my room for the night. Later guys!"

I came to my senses enough at the comment to wave a quick goodnight to Rascal before she retreated to her bedroom. I closed my eyes, leaned forward to put my elbows on my knees and ran my fingers through my hair. Angel reached over, gave my back a quick rub and then kissed my temple. She left me sitting there alone without another word. She knew me well enough to know I needed to be alone.

I caught myself wondering if Rascal and Kayla ever would split up, they definitely seemed happy enough. Usually by a month in, which is roughly where they were at, Ras was beginning to distance herself a little at a time. This one appeared to be sticking and it sucked some serious balls. I forced myself up off the couch and flipped the TV off then stood there.

The only thing that reached my mind was what I usually got up to on a Friday night. Since I couldn't think of any reason to not go do exactly what I always did, I grabbed my keys and headed for the door. I drove like I was on autopilot and finally ended up in Old Town Scottsdale. I made my way into the first crowded bar I found, weaving my way to the bar and ordering a drink. Glass in hand I scanned the crowd several times. I finally settled on a girl who looked sufficiently tipsy and worked my way through the crowd and over to her.

I wasn't in the mood for a lot of chat tonight so I intended to get this done with as little conversation as I could possibly manage. I slipped up behind her on the dance floor after making sure she didn't look to be there with anyone and started dancing with her. She was buzzed enough when my arm slid around her waist, my hand settling on her stomach, she looked over her shoulder and grinned at me. I felt her weight against me as she leaned back, her shoulder length brown hair tickled the tops of my shoulder and the side of my neck.

I pressed my hand into her stomach to pull her back against me, not sure if she realized in the dark of the club and through the fog of alcohol I wasn't a man. Normally I didn't really care and even now it only niggled at me a little bit as I leaned in and brushed my lips up her neck to her ear. I couldn't hear the soft purr she let out over the thumping bass in the place but I felt it. It rumbled against both my hand and the front of my body as it vibrated through her. My hand traveled up her stomach and brushed over her right breast roughly, making her bite her lower lip as she turned her head toward me.

"You having fun dancing or you wanna get out of here?"

The response she gave was to grab my hand and start for the door. I wasn't about to ask her if she was sure. I followed her outside and around to the side of the building, letting her fall into my arms and push me into the side of the building. I grinned as she pressed the length of her body against mine and went right along with the kiss she started.

Everything was progressing exactly as it always did and I knew it was only a matter of time before she was naked and begging me for more. My pulse quickened and my breathing became ragged and choppy as I felt her hands slip under my shirt. Her skin contacted mine and sent a shiver down my spine. One hand changed direction, heading back down my stomach. Her fingertips slipped under the waistband of my pants as her tongue worked past my lips.

Those two very intense points of contact should have rendered me putty in her hands. Instead they somehow brought everything around me into sharp focus and snapped my senses away from her. What should have felt good suddenly felt completely wrong as an image of a completely different brunette I was trying to keep out of my mind slipped into it without my consent. I shoved the girl away and stared at her as if she was some kind of alien and then shook my head.

"Fuck. I can't do this. I'm sorry."

I tugged my shirt back into place and turned on my heel, heading out of the alley and back to my car. I had never had that happen to me before. I was at a loss. I eased into the drivers' seat, started it, crossed my arms on top of the steering wheel and leaned my head against them. This thing was getting serious and there didn't seem to be anything I could do to make it end and reverse the effect it was having on me. I sat there for several minutes until a security guard tapped on my window and told me I needed to move.

I gave him a small nod, put the car in gear and left the lot, not even sure where I was headed. I didn't know if I could handle being at home. Being right there, a flight of stairs away from the woman who was sending my emotional state into a tailspin would be too damn hard. I drove without any real idea of where I was heading, needing to be somewhere quiet where I could think, maybe even sleep. I finally pulled into a darkened parking lot. I didn't really giving a damn where I was as crawled into the backseat of my car. I needed to try and make my brain be quiet and get some sleep, look at this with a fresh perspective. At least I hoped it would be fresh.

After an hour staring out the window I finally drifted off. The sleep I fell into was fitful and run through with dreams. Dreams about Rascal. Dreams which made me ache in places I wasn't used too. I had spent years getting into the habit of dealing with aches stemming from sexual tension but this, it was new. I rarely got attached to anyone, and by rarely I mean once in my life and it had turned out terrible. The single experience had colored my thoughts and outlook on relationships and commitment.

I had done my best to stay well clear of those things. I was better off on my own, not having to trust someone with my heart, with my happiness. If the girl all those years ago had taught me anything it was I couldn't trust people with my heart no matter what they said, regardless of what my gut told me. I had managed to stay clear of making the same mistake again but now I could feel myself sliding right back into those feelings. I hated it but not because it made me feel like I had failed in my attempts but because I was actually considering following through with what I was feeling. What was stopping me was a blonde roadblock named Kayla.

CHAPTER SEVEN

Saturday, March 21st, 2009 – Scottsdale, Arizona

I woke with a stunted stretch and knocked my head against the inside of my back door. I groaned and rubbed the sore spot as I remembered where I was and how I ended up there in the first place. The realization made me release another groan. I was losing it and I needed to find it and get it back together, fast. I popped my back door and liberated myself from the back seat, allowing a few moments for my back to protest its' overnight treatment.

A good, solid stretch and some bending and twisting later and I dropped into the driver's seat and started toward home. It was early but still late enough that the only one home should be James. I should have a chance to shower and grab something to eat. My mind was still attempting to wrap around what had transpired outside the club the night before. My head kicked up a steady throbbing so I allowed the thoughts to drift away, deciding I could deal with them later.

I reached over, flipped on the radio and glared at the cheesy love song blaring out of my speakers. I punched the scan button several times, finding more of the same. I wondered if the DJs knew what I was dealing with and were screwing with me. I knew there was no way it was the case but sometimes it was nice to have somewhere to direct agitation. I growled and slapped at the power button for the damn thing, shutting it off in the middle of All I Ever Wanted by Basshunter. Somehow I kept my head free of my situation and its implications for the remainder of the drive.

The silence in my brain held as I pulled into the driveway, finding only one car left. I was almost glad I might be able to have a nice, normal chat with James. I parked, slid out of the vehicle and made my way inside. I found her sitting at the island on a bar stool, eating toast and hunched over a server mapping book. I caught the flash of blue on her Bluetooth headphones when it flickered to say they were charged and raised an eyebrow. Too easy, far too easy. I grinned and eased up behind her, knowing she hadn't heard me come in and lightly poked her in both sides with my index fingers.

"Holy shit!"

I laughed as she jumped a couple feet and yanked the headphones off, turning on me with a glare. I held both hands in front of me in surrender as I backed up a couple steps. I attempted to look apologetic for what I had done but the smirk clinging to my lips gave me away.

"You suck."

"Not recently but thanks for the glowing recommendation."

She narrowed her eyes and flung the half slice of toast in her hand at me as I laughed and side stepped the flying breakfast bread.

"Where were you last night? No, wait, maybe I don't want to know."

She smirked at me and the memory of what had happened in the alley the night before flooded back. I leaned hard against the wall behind me and wiped a hand down my face with a heavy sigh.

"Uh oh, that doesn't sound good. Wanna talk about it?"

"No but thanks anyway. Had a weird night and I think I need to sleep it off, ya know?"

She nodded and then turned to flip the book she'd been studying closed and tossed it to me. I caught it and raised an eyebrow as I looked at it then glanced back up at her.

"New client, old ass servers they refuse to upgrade. So we get to revisit mapping for XP."

I rolled my eyes and grumbled, not looking forward to brushing up on something I'd probably never use again after this client. James grinned and held her hands up in front of her in surrender as she grabbed her keys.

"Don't take it out on me dude, the boss and I tried to talk some sense into them. Maybe you'll have better luck. If you ever come in and, I don't know, do some work or something like it?"

I narrowed my eyes and flipped her off, dropping my hand as she brushed past me, heading for the front door. She called out a goodbye which I waved off before wandering to my room. I dropped the ridiculous book on my desk before flopping onto the bed. I'd gotten a few short and very crappy hours of sleep and I decided a nap sounded amazing. I kicked off my shoes, folded my arms behind my head and closed my eyes. I thought falling asleep would be easy but as it turned out, my mind still had other ideas.

Thoughts of Rascal and her new girlfriend whirled through my mind, followed shortly by snippets of my conversation with Angel. I knew my best friend might be right but it didn't mean I knew what to do. She thought I should be pushing for something to happen with Rascal but I had my reasons for believing I was right. The last thing I wanted was to weasel myself between her and the new girl and end up with her asking 'what if?' down the line. If I let myself be honest, I didn't want anything we might have to start out as the mistake she thought she might have made.

I huffed loudly, opened my eyes, and sat up. After I pushed myself back against the headboard I let the back of my head bounce lightly off the wall several times. I was giving myself a headache but I had hope the jarring would shake something worthwhile loose in my damn brain. After two solid minutes I finally stopped. Not only had it not worked but my left eye had developed a small twitch. I shifted and dropped my feet to the floor, my elbows on my knees, hands rising to cover my face.

"Why are you doing this to yourself? Why? Because you're a moron. You want her, more than that you love her. You know it, you've admitted it and now you're terrified of it."

I had regressed to talking to myself in my empty room which suddenly seemed very sad. I exhaled sharply, rubbed my face a couple times and then pushed up to my feet. I needed to do something, anything. I couldn't sit and question myself all day, it would end up driving me completely crazy. I shoved my feet into my sneakers and left my bedroom, needing a distraction, preferably something noisy where I couldn't hear myself think.

I left the house and climbed back into my so very recently vacated vehicle, backing out of the driveway before actually deciding where I was heading. I drove with no destination in mind until I realized I had landed myself within blocks of an old regular spot. I smiled as I changed lanes and pulled into the parking lot at Cosmo Dog Park. I parked, slipped from the car and claimed a spot on a bench near the lake but outside the fenced area. It had been years since I'd owned a dog but I had always found peace and comfort at the park.

I had been in the park right at five minutes by the time I checked my watch and realized I was already smiling. The expression brightened further when a thigh-height fluff of a dog barreled over with a tennis ball in his mouth. He dropped the soggy yellow thing at my feet and then shook, soaking me from head to toe. I laughed, shook the lake from my arms then picked the ball up and threw it back out into the water. The black poodle tore right back into the water after what I could only believe was a favorite toy as someone sat next to me on the bench.

"Sorry he drenched you, he prefers to shake on people whenever possible."

The recently familiar voice made me tense slightly as I looked over to see Kayla seated beside me. I cleared my throat as the dog charged back over and repeated the process all over again, drop, shake and then wait for the toss. I ripped my gaze from the blonde sitting next to me and threw the ball for the dog again.

"He yours?"

"Yeah. Braxton! Come here boy."

I nodded but kept quiet as the dog removed himself from the water, ball once again in his mouth and trotted over to us. My brain was putting together several snarky comments about the fact this woman had a poodle but I knew I wouldn't voice a single one. Instead I stared out at the water, watching the small silver fish at the edge nibble at algae and hoping Kayla would leave.

"You have a dog? I remember seeing one at the house but I could have sworn someone said he belonged to Jamie."

It took five or six seconds for my brain to kick in and process her question but then I shook my head without looking at her.

"No, I haven't owned one for years. Pippen does belong to James."

"I couldn't imagine being without one. Had them as long as I can remember. Brax here just turned four, he was a birthday present from my mom. And Argo... Where is that dog?"

I glanced over at her as she scanned the group of dogs playing in and around the lake. I caught the smile as it lit up her face when she apparently found her other dog. She brought her fingers to her mouth and gave a sharp whistle, getting the attention of half the dogs in the area. One broke away from the bunch and ran toward the bench we had taken over full steam. My eyes widened as the hundred-plus pound dog launched himself at Kayla and promptly rolled onto his back across her lap, and mine in the process. She scratched his belly as she baby talked to him, telling him he was a good boy and I realized the dog only had three legs, the front left having been removed at the shoulder.

"This is Argo. He's six. I rescued him five years ago after someone in my complex threw him off a third story balcony. Shattered his leg but he's fine other than that. Aren't you, boy?"

The muscled, tailless dog wiggled on her lap and covered her face in slobbery kisses. My heart seized uncomfortably as I realized that when she wasn't hanging all over Rascal, I didn't hate Kayla at all. She seemed like a genuinely sweet person and I hated myself for wishing the two of them would break up. I took a deep breath and forced my gaze back out across the water before exhaling slowly.

"Hey, are you okay?"

"Uh, yeah. Fine."

I wasn't about to tell her about my internal crisis, which she happened to play a starring role in. Talk about causing even more problems.

"I know we don't really know each other but if you need to talk, I have a free ear."

"Why would you want to listen to my problems?"

She was silent for a few beats and then I heard her sigh and felt the bench shift slightly as she moved beside me.

"Lux, I really like Rebecca. More than I think she actually knows. I'm doing the best I can to try and fit into a group of people who have known each other longer than I've lived in this state. It's, well honestly, really intimidating. The way she talks about you I got the feeling you two were really close but, I hardly see you around. Makes me worry that I've done or said something that's made you hate me. If that's the case, give me a chance to fix it. Please. I don't want to lose her."

My heart shattered at the emotion in her plea and it cemented the idea I'd had. I couldn't get between her and Rascal. I bit down hard on the inside of my cheek to keep the tears beginning to mist my eyes at bay and took a steadying breath.

"It's nothing like that, Kayla. I'm... Just busy right now. Look, I should probably go. I just needed to clear my head a little but I have things to get done."

I stood, stretched as the dogs ran off to play again and ran right into Kayla as I turned to retreat to my car. She mumbled an apology and sidestepped out of my way, allowing me to vacate her vicinity without any theatrics. I returned to my car, pulled out of the lot and made for the nearest church, knowing I had a fifty-fifty shot the lot would be empty. The first church looked packed but the second was a ghost town and I parked sideways across three spaces and dropped my head onto my steering wheel. I told myself I wouldn't cry, not willing to give in to the emotions still warring within me. I lost the fight in less than three minutes and felt the warmth streaking down my cheeks against my will.

"Damn it!"

I slammed my palm against my steering wheel as I shouted at nothing and everything all at once. I was an emotional wreck and I doubted it would be getting better any time soon. I let the tears run themselves out. I cycled between sobbing and yelling at nothing from the confines of my car for the next forty minutes. Eventually I had nothing left to cry out, drained emotionally, mentally and physically from the last couple hours of my day. I'd had enough but the thought of going home and running into either of them, Rascal or Kayla, made my heart ache and my head throb.

I eventually gave in and made my way home, slipping in and finding the house dark, empty and blessedly silent. I shuffled to my room and collapsed on my bed fully clothed, not even bothering to kick off my shoes. I turned my face into my pillow as the tears started up again. I hadn't thought there were any left to escape but apparently I'd been wrong. Sleep didn't find me for another hour and by then I was thoroughly exhausted.

CHAPTER EIGHT

Friday, April 10th, 2009 – San Tan Valley, Arizona
I pulled up to the house after a hectic sixteen-hour day to find several familiar vehicles parked out front. I managed a smile as I thought about starting my weekend hanging out with my friends. The process had been made easier when I rather forcefully told myself that Kayla was a decent human being and might actually be good for Rascal. It allowed me to accept my friends happiness rather than be jealous of her new flame. I still wouldn't claim to be happy about the situation but I'd made it bearable at least.

I stepped into the house and followed the sounds of laughter into the living room, grinning when I saw everyone gathered watching a movie. I returned greetings as they were directed my way and dropped onto the couch, laying across James and Angel's laps. They both made 'oh god you're fat, get off me' noises then Angel shoved me off onto the rug with a laugh.

"Well, that was just rude."

I rolled onto my back, pushed myself up onto my elbows and looked up at Angel as she smirked at me.

"It was not rude Lux, it was a reflex."

"Reflex?"

"Yep. Preservation of my poor little legs against your giant ass."

I scoffed dramatically as if she'd hurt my feelings, hand over my heart and mouth hanging open which caused everyone to erupt in laughter again.

"I'll have you know that I have a perfectly average-sized ass. I spend a lot of time pretending to go to the gym to keep it that way."

The very matter-of-fact statement made Dani laugh so hard she spit soda several feet into the room. Zara shook her head, James rolled her eyes and Angel laughed so hard she fell off the couch and landed on top of me. I let out a hefty 'oof!' then smacked at her butt until she rolled off of me, settling between my body and the coffee table.

"Damn Angel, that was a little rough even for me. Besides, I prefer to be on top."

I laughed when she punched me in the shoulder and called me a pervert, delivering a weak kick to her ankle in response. The move fired off a highly childish round of slaps, punches, kicks, and tickling. I waved her off when she had tickled me to the point I could barely breathe. She rolled to her side and laid her head on my shoulder as our laughter died down and I wrapped my arm around her. I stared at the ceiling as my heart rate returned to normal, my fingertips absently tracing patterns on her upper arm. The conversation my appearance had interrupted picked up again but I closed my eyes, only half listening since I'd missed the beginning of it anyway.

Ten minutes later, right in the middle of a heated discussion about whether Voyager or Deep Space Nine was better, the front door slammed. We all jumped at the sound, Angel and I sitting up and looking toward the entry. Rascal stood in the foyer, anger etched into her features, car keys in one hand, phone in her other and Bluetooth flashing its little blue flickers from her left ear.

"God, how many times do I have to tell you I don't want to talk about it?"

Her voice pitched at the end of her sentence and it put us on high alert. She was even more pissed than she looked. Angel and I scrambled off the floor and settled on the couch with James, watching our friend's posture stiffen as she glare at the front door. Her breathing was harsh and rapid, her chest rising and falling in quick succession and I knew she was trying to calm herself. We caught her side of the conversation, listening intently and hoping it would tell us what had her so angry.

"No, I'm so over this. I can't take it anymore... You're right, you don't understand. You'll never understand and I'm sick and fucking tired of trying to explain it to you... Because I can't just say what you want to hear if I don't mean it, Kayla!"

The mention of the adorable blonde Rascal had been dating for the last couple months made us glance around at each other. I couldn't help wondering what they were fighting about, though her wording gave me a clue, I wasn't about to leap to any conclusions.

"Don't even try to guilt me into giving in... I seriously don't understand how you can be mad at me for being honest with you. Wouldn't it be worse if I'd lied and you found out five months from now? Well what do you want me to do? No, not a chance... You know what Kayla? You can take your guilt trips, your tears, and your pushy crap and fuck right off."

She ended the call, threw her Bluetooth and phone across the room then shocked us when she punched the front door. Rascal hadn't punched anything in well over a year and the fact she had been pushed so far meant things were bad. Angel vaulted off the couch and closed the distance between the living room and foyer in a few long strides. Rascal turned to lean her back against the door, sliding down to the floor by the time Angel reached her, head hanging. Angel crouched beside her, speaking in hushed tones low enough I couldn't make out what she was saying. Five minutes passed before she pulled herself up off the floor, gave Rascal's shoulder a squeeze and returned to the rest of us.

I met her gaze as she walked back into the room and she shook her head, letting me know it was up to Rascal to talk if she wanted to do so. I nodded my understanding before the sound of shoes on tile drew my attention toward the front door. I was off the couch by the time Rascal made it to the living room, ready to help in any way I could. I hadn't expected her to acknowledge any of us after a blowout like the one she'd just been through so it shocked me when she fell into my arms.

I went rigid for a split second as I tried to decide what to do then remembered this was Rascal and wrapped my arms around her. Her arms tightened around my waist as she sobbed against my shoulder and I could only imagine I hosted a spectacular deer-in-the-headlights expression. The rest of our friends decided she'd be more likely to talk without a crowd and silently made their exits from the house. It left the two of us standing alone in the living room. I let myself relax once no one was there to witness my fall from the pedestal of pride I lived atop. I closed my eyes, leaned my cheek against her head and rubbed her back in slow circles. Her crying eventually slowed to a few hiccupped sobs then stopped completely.

"You wanna talk about it?"

She shook her head against my shoulder as she sniffled and the sound combined with the wet shoulder of my shirt broke me. I'd never seen her fall apart so completely and all I wanted to do was fix it. She gave me a nudge and I backed up until my calves hit the edge of the couch then sat down. She crawled up beside me, never losing contact as she curled against my side. I searched for something to say, some way to let her know everything would be okay. Instead I reached for her hand, the one she had used to assault the front door.

I lifted it and checked her knuckles carefully, making sure nothing was broken. They seemed to be fine so I started to drop it back to where it had been. I paused and, against what should have been my better judgement, lifted it and brushed my lips over the reddened knuckles. I considered speaking again as I returned her hand to my hip but still had no words. Before I found any the sniffling stopped and her breathing deepened, leveling out into the steady rise and fall of someone dead asleep. I allowed a small smile to tilt the corners of my lips.

I scooted myself around until I was stretched out on my back with the smaller woman tucked in against my side. She moved a bit, getting comfortable again and then settled down with her head on my chest, one leg thrown over mine. She rested her arm across my stomach and mumbled something in her sleep. I risked dropping a gentle kiss on the top of her head before I closed my eyes. The long days I'd been putting in lately caught up with me and I was asleep in minutes. For the first time in longer than I could remember my sleep was restful. It was free of weird dreams and had no relived memories that made my chest tight.

CHAPTER NINE

Saturday, April 11th, 2009 – San Tan Valley, Arizona

A light tap on my forehead woke me up. I eased my eyes open against the light I was sure shouldn't be penetrating my curtains. Once my vision focused two things became clear, I wasn't in my bedroom and it had been Angel tapping my forehead. I offered her a sleepy half smile and then yawned, stopping mid-stretch when I remembered Rascal curled against my side. I looked down, finding her still wrapped around me and sleeping so deeply she probably wouldn't wake up for a while. I turned my attention back up to Angel and she grinned at me.

"What?"

"Nothing. James and I are headed out for a bit. See if you can get her to talk when she wakes up."

I let my gaze flicker to Rascal quickly before returning it to Angel and gave her a small nod. She really did need to talk about what had happened the night before. Whether or not she would want to talk about it with me I wouldn't know until I tried. James bounded down the stairs and motioned for Angel to follow her. She looked over her shoulder, waving at me as they left for some normal Saturday running around. Once they were gone and the house was still once more, I closed my eyes again and dozed off again. I twitched myself awake, startled by the feel of a kiss being pressed to my cheek. I opened my eyes and looked down at Rascal.

"Hey you. How ya feeling?"

"Hey. I'm... Okay."

I raised a skeptical eyebrow at her, not sure I should let it go after what I had witnessed a few hours earlier. I mulled it over for about ten seconds before I started to say something, deciding how best to push the subject without upsetting her. I never got the chance to form the words since she spoke up again before they formed properly in my mind.

"Well, maybe okay is a bit strong."

"Ready to talk about it?"

"Am I ready? No. Do I need to? Definitely."

"I'm all ears hon."

The pressure of her chest against my stomach increased as she took a deep breath and I assumed she was preparing herself to explain her phone conversation.

"Kayla told me she loved me."

My heart stopped and missed at least three beats when her words hit me. I choked on the breath I tried to take when my body decided to work again but she thankfully didn't seem to notice.

"She did? Wow."

My voice had dropped to a strained sort of whimper and I hated how pathetic it sounded. The idea of the woman in my arms, curled against me, telling someone else she loved them hurt more than I would have expected. My chest ached, my eyes burned as they misted over and my jaw tensed to keep it under control so she wouldn't notice. I tried to recall her side of the conversation so I could piece together why they'd been fighting after what she'd told me. The whole thing was a jumble since all my senses had wanted to process at the time was Rascal hurting. My entire being had wanted to jump in and make her feel better.

"Yeah, thing is, I just stood there and stared at her for a minute and then I hugged her. Then she got pissed because I didn't say it back. I tried to tell her I've never believed in saying those words to someone just because they said it first. I want to wait until I actually feel it. She thought that was an excuse then she blew up at me. I walked away, she called, I answered, we fought and you guys heard the end of the fight."

"Damn."

"Right?"

"So where does that leave you two?"

A guilty twinge shot through my heart when I momentarily hoped they were broken up for good and I might have a shot. I immediately pushed the thought aside in favor of making sure she wouldn't fall apart on me.

"It leaves us nowhere. We're done. I can't be with someone who expects me to tell them I love them just because they felt like saying it. That's not me Lux. You know that."

"Yeah, I do."

It was the truth, I had known her for years and she was nothing if not independent and confident in her beliefs. One of those beliefs was that people used the word love too liberally. She'd been telling us for years now that she would say it when she felt it and not a minute before. I respected her for the outlook but couldn't remember if I'd ever told her.

"What are you thinking about so hard?"

Her voice snapped me out of my thoughts and I smiled down at her with a shake of my head.

"Just trying to remember if I've ever told you how much I respect and admire you for sticking to all of this even when it seems like the world is telling you to cave."

"Nope, you haven't."

"Well now I am. I think I feel the same way. Not that I've been in a situation where someone told me they loved me in the last, oh, ever."

I chuckled, the slight movement of my shirt under her cheek telling me she was smiling at my comment. A smile was good, it meant progress and maybe she'd be able to move past the whole ordeal after all.

"You're problem is that you don't let people reach that point because you don't believe you deserve to be loved."

I shrugged because even though she was right there was no way I would tell her, she'd never let me forget it. She dropped the subject, grabbed the remote and flipped on the TV, our long time signal ending a difficult conversation. We laid together silently, watching *The Fifth Element* and holding each other until we both needed to eat.

CHAPTER TEN

Sunday, April 12th, 2009 – San Tan Valley, Arizona

I sat at the table attempting to enjoy my lunch but Angel sat across from me grinning like the Cheshire cat. I tried to ignore her, staring at the chips left on my plate but the attention finally got under my skin.

"Oh my... What?"

"So you two spent the whole night on the couch together, huh?"

"Really? That's what you're interrupting my lunch for?"

"Mmhmm."

"Angel, she and I have spent nights together before you know."

"Not like that."

"Granted, she was upset and pretty drained."

She crossed her arms on the tabletop and raised an eyebrow as she leaned in closer as if she couldn't believe I was so dense

"I mean falling asleep cuddled up together without having sex first."

I started to argue with her but then I stopped and actually thought about it. She was right, Rascal and I had never fallen asleep in the same space without having sex first. Not that I could remember. I suddenly felt like I'd been using her like I used those one night stands I kicked out before breakfast.

"Wow. I'm disgusting. How do you guys put up with me?"

She barked out a laugh with a shake of her head and then covered my hand with her own. She trailed her thumb over my knuckles for a few beats before she looked up again and smiled at me.

"You aren't disgusting and we love ya. Well, maybe you're a little disgusting."

I narrowed my eyes and threw a chip at her as we both broke into laughter. I picked up my plate, pushed my chair back, and walked over to drop the dish in the sink. I turned and leaned against the counter, my focus back on Angel as she joined me, leaning on the counter across from me.

"Angel. I think I'm tired of being disgusting. I've been running around this city playing the field for years and all I've accomplished is making half the women in the state hate me."

"Half the women in the state? Don't we think highly of our numbers?"

I grinned at her and chuckled then ran my hands over my face and up through my hair, linking my fingers at the back of my head. I stretched, arching my back over the sink then righted myself to continue the conversation.

"Okay maybe half was a stretch but at the very least every women I've slept with. I'm hated, Angel. Do you have any idea what that feels like?"

"Not really but if someone does hate me I'm probably busy ignoring them. Plus, you've slept with most of us, we don't hate you."

"Yeah well, you have time left to change your mind. I'm sure I can think of brand new depraved and filthy things to expose you all to."

She snorted which made me grin and then she pushed off the counter and pulled my hands from behind my head. Once they were free she tugged me closer and wrapped my arms around her waist, hers falling around my neck so she could hug me. She squeezed and I reciprocated the gesture with a heavy sigh. My behavior the last few years hadn't earned me brownie points with anyone who had been witness to them and my friends had seen more than most people. We ignored the door opening and then closing again but the sound of someone clearing their throat behind us ended the hug as we both turned to face our guest.

"Uh, I'll make myself scarce."

I gave Angel a pleading look as she shrugged and removed herself from the room as quickly as she could manage.

"Hey Courtney."

"Hey Lux. I was hoping we could talk."

"I'd like that but don't you still hate me?"

She sighed, her shoulders rising and then drooping with the action then looked up at me.

"I couldn't hate you. I was angry and hurt and you were the easiest person to take it out on. That was really crappy of me and... I'm sorry."

I considered pinching myself to make sure I hadn't dreamed her apology since I hadn't considered deserving it. I stood in silence and let the words hang between us, giving them time to sink in.

"Don't be, I know how I come across and I don't blame you. I just wish you'd spoken up earlier. Courtney you can talk to me, we may not always agree but we are friends and the last thing I want to do is hurt you. Okay?"

She nodded as a tear slid down her cheek so I reached over and wiped it away then folded her into a hug. I smiled when she hugged me back and I gave her a squeeze before letting her go and taking a step back.

"Are we done fighting now? Because fighting with any of you guys sucks and makes me feel like I'm cutting off my own arm."

She giggled and nodded as she wiped away the last of the tears clinging to her cheeks and then gave me a playful slap on my shoulder.

"I'll try harder to just talk to you all."

"And I promise to do everything I can short of out and telling Jamie how you feel about her to fix this."

"Really?"

"Of course. Hell, I think you two would make a cute couple."

She turned bright read and ducked her head as a shy smile worked its way across her features, setting the twinkle in the corner of her eye alight. She really was a sweet person and I knew if I could get James to pay attention to her they could have a shot at something real. The question was how to make it happen. I would be putting as much effort as I could manage into the endeavor once I sorted my own shit out. I had to get a handle on my feelings for Rascal but I didn't have the faintest idea where to begin. I said goodbye to Courtney and walked her to the front door as Angel walked back in.

"So?"

"We're good. She apologized and so did I. I'm gonna work on James and see if I can get through to her about Courtney without giving the whole thing away."

"Well, good luck with that Sergeant Subtle."

"Thanks Private pain-in-my-ass."

We burst out laughing, letting it run its three minute course then I moved back to the kitchen to load up the dishwasher. There was so much going on in my head I didn't realize Angel had left me alone in the kitchen until I turned around to say something to her and found an empty room. She knew me well and understood that if she was there I would chatter at her instead of dealing with the issues at hand. Being the amazing best friend she was, she'd left me to sort myself out and gone about her business elsewhere. Perfect.

CHAPTER ELEVEN

Saturday, May 22nd, 2009 – San Tan Valley, Arizona

I stepped inside and kicked the door closed behind me, heading toward the kitchen. I dropped the groceries I'd picked up on the counter, tossing the cold items in the fridge or freezer as needed and leaving the rest for later. I had just dropped my keys on the counter when fingers closed around my wrist and I turned to look at Rascal. A smile spread across my face at the little grin she was flashing me and I cocked an eyebrow at her.

"Need something?"

"Yeah actually. I need to talk to you, come here."

She gave my wrist a tug and I followed her across the room and down the hall to my bedroom. She kicked the door closed and I opened my mouth to ask her what she needed to talk about when she beat me to it.

"I've been doing a lot of thinking since I broke up with Kayla."

"Oh?"

"Yes. I realized these relationships I land in never last long, a handful of weeks, sometimes months if I can stand them that long and then, poof, they end."

"Uh huh."

"Seriously Lux. You can't tell me you haven't noticed."

"No, I noticed I just chose to keep it to myself."

She grinned and shook her head at me, running her hand through her hair before she spoke again.

"Well, I decided I should talk to my friends about it. I started with Zara and Dani since I don't live with them and they helped me gain some insight. It still didn't fill in all the gaps so I went to James who helped more than I expected. Yesterday I sat down with Angel for a couple hours and thought I had a pretty good grasp on the situation. Then I considered talking to you about it."

Her thought ended, leaving me grasping at where she could be heading with the comment. I looked at her for some filler but she was leaning against my bedroom wall staring at her shoes.

"Ras?"

"When I thought about it my head would get fuzzy, my chest felt tight, and I had to sit down. I couldn't bring myself to talk to you about why it never lasted with those other girls."

My brow furrowed as I gave her a questioning look, hoping she would be continuing on to tell me what I had obviously missed.

"Why not? I mean, do you think you can't trust me or that I won't be honest with you?"

She looked up, her eyes meeting mine and I lost myself in their chocolate depths for a five count before I shook my head to bring the room back into focus. The smile had returned to her face and I could make out the faint pink tinting of a blush beginning on her cheeks. Apparently she'd caught what had happened, not that I'd been subtle about it.

"Nothing like that. I know I can trust you, I actually trust you more than anyone."

"But?"

"Not but as much as however... I didn't know how to tell you that all those relationships failed because I was waiting on something, someone, I didn't think I could ever have... I was waiting on you, Lux."

My mouth moved as I tried desperately to make words come out of it but nothing wanted to cooperate. I got out the beginnings of a 'what?' but the full word never had a chance to come to fruition. She pushed away from the wall and threw her arms around my neck. If that had been the extent of her movement I might have found a few words but then she threw me completely off-balance. She kissed me. I froze for the span of six racing heartbeats then my eyes fluttered closed and my arms slipped around her waist.

The moment I returned her kiss she melted against me and despite the fact we'd kissed before this time felt different. There was no hesitation on her end. Her actions and reactions instantaneous and genuine. It was like she was meeting me emotionally rather than the purely physical interactions we'd always shared before. My breath caught in my chest when her fingers found the inch-long hair at the back of my head and trailed through it. I gripped the back of her shirt but made no move to get under the fabric or remove it which prompted her to sigh against my cheek.

Her tongue traced along my lips and I didn't think when I parted them for her, only reacted. The jolt that flared through me when her tongue met mine left me flushed and tingling from head to toe and I knew everything about this contact was new, different, better. When she finally pulled back enough to take a deep breath she kept as much contact as she could, her arms still wrapped around my neck. I held onto her like a lifeline in an open ocean. I was terrified if I let her go the whole scene would fade and turn out to be nothing but a dream.

"Lux."

The whisper of my name as it escaped her and brushed across my skin made me shudder. A smile tugged at the corners of her lips when she felt it. I stood there, not sure what to do next since this looked nothing like my usual interactions with her. She moved first, turning us and backing me against the edge of my bed until I sat down. I looked up at her as she reached up to run her fingers through my short hair and the buzzing in my brain slowly slipped away. The clearing of my mind and awareness of every second that passed between us made me stop her hand as it went for the hem of my shirt.

Her brow knit in confusion at the interruption until I kicked my shoes off, prompted her to do the same, and pulled her onto the bed. I leaned back, taking her with me as I stretched out and rested my head on the pillows. I guided her up beside me. She settled in against my right side. My body erupted in a wave of shivers as her hand slipped under the bottom edge of my shirt. The bed beside me shifted as she moved, swinging one leg over my hips and sitting up. She looked down from where she sat straddling me and we both smiled. I realized I was actually nervous.

I sat up when she tugged on my shirt, letting her pull it over my head before I lifted hers off. Her fingertips tickled along the tops of my shoulders as I trailed mine lightly up her sides. We had been in this very situation more times than I could count. I still couldn't shake the weird feeling this was the first time. My fingers found the bottom edge of her bra, followed it and then I unhooked it and moved to hook my fingers into the straps. It fell away easily and I dropped it on the floor with our shirts, mine joining it a few breaths later.

Our lips reconnected and the rest of our clothes were shed before I had time to register them being removed. She pushed me down to the mattress and I stunned myself when I didn't fight her for dominance. The discovery that I didn't mind her taking the lead threatened to halt our progress until her lips touched my neck. All thoughts of arguing or trying to take control of the situation to prove a point were wiped away with the contact. My fingers tangled into her hair as she kissed her way down my neck and across my collarbone. I let go of my insane need for control and let her move at her own pace.

I pulled in a sharp breath when her tongue made first contact with my left nipple and closed my eyes. She seemed to be treating this encounter differently as well, taking her time teasing me, something she had never done before. I had to admit, I was enjoying it even though I had always been firm on my belief of hating teasing. Before this I had found it tedious, time wasting but the tide had shifted and I was thoroughly enjoying myself. She kissed her way back up my neck, her right hand making its way down my body. Our lips reconnected as her hand drifted between my legs, my whimper muffled by her kiss.

I followed her lead once my brain kicked in, one hand easing between our bodies, tracing a gentle trail south. I ghosted my fingertips over the clean shaven skin, cupping her as one finger teased along her lips. She shivered against me and I used the movement to slide a fingertip over her clit, she responded by doing the same. The kiss was broken as my head fell back against my pillow and I barely bit back the moan trying to break free. She didn't attempt to stifle hers, letting it reach my ears as she dropped her head to my shoulder.

She took her time circling my clit slowly, building the tension already coiled in my lower body. It took every bit of willpower I had to keep from whining at her, begging her to stop the teasing and get on with it. She needed this, so did I if I was being honest with myself. I smiled and pulled my lower lip between my teeth as she raised her head to look into my eyes. I stared into those beautiful brown depths I knew so well. There was no doubting it now, I really was completely in love with this woman. This crazy, goofy, caring, exciting woman who had been my friend for so many years.

I used my free hand to tuck her hair behind her ear, my

breathing hitching, losing its steady rhythm as her touch worked its magic on me. I brushed a light kiss over her lips and spoke before I could think about my words and stop myself.

"I love you, Rebecca."

Her eyes misted over as she smiled and she chose that moment to stop teasing me, sliding two fingers inside me as she pressed her lips to my ear.

"I love you, too."

I woke hours later, my arms wrapped around another body, my face buried against her neck through a sweep of chocolate brown hair. I smiled as I nuzzled my way up to her ear, kissing back down the edge of her jaw until she stirred. She stretched and I loosened my grip on her so she could turn over and face me. A smile took over my face in response to the one painted across hers. I brushed the hair off her forehead and dropped a light kiss where my fingers had touched. After the night we had shared we had a lot to talk about but I worried about what the night meant, or didn't mean.

Part of me wanted to leave it alone, not bring it up and let things play out on their own. I knew we couldn't really do things that way though. After the things I had done, the lifestyle I'd been living, we would need to figure out what everything meant. She deserved it and I couldn't deny her whatever she needed to be comfortable with the situation.

"So where does this leave us?"

My thoughts paused when she spoke and I reached down to link my fingers with hers. I raised her hand, kissing each of her knuckles before I answered her.

"Where do you want it to leave us?"

"What do you mean?"

"Becca, you know my history and I can understand if that makes you want to call this a one night thing and walk away."

"Is that what you want?"

I could hear the disappointment and confusion in her voice and as much as it hurt me the pain etched on her face was even worse.

"Of course not. I just don't want you to think you have to do anything. Do I want this to mean something? Yes. Would I like the chance to be with you, actually with you in a relationship? Definitely. But it's your choice. Believe me I would understand if you don't want to try and wean me off all the bullshit I've spent years getting used to doing."

The smile returned to her face with a small chuckle and it gave me hope.

"Lux, of course I want to try. Do you think I would have said any of the things I did last night if I wasn't looking for something serious with you? Did you block out me telling you I loved you?"

"Of course I didn't. And I hope you know how much it meant to me, and that I meant it when I said it."

"I know you did. The question is, are you ready for something serious? Can you handle it?"

I didn't actually answer her question, simply nodded and pulled her into a kiss. The night had been amazing but the morning was already proving to be even better. I didn't know where the future would take us but I did know wherever I ended up, I wanted to be there with Rebecca. The feeling was new, a little awkward but I found myself liking it. I broke the kiss and rolled over, pulling her arms around me and settling back in. I wanted to stay in bed a little longer before we had to face the rest of the world, and our friends. She seemed to agree because she tightened her arms and threw a leg over my hip as she nuzzled the back of my neck.

I had almost slipped back to sleep when a door slamming jolted me awake again. My brow furrowed as the thud of something hitting the wall sounded from the other room. I turned over to face Rascal and raised an eyebrow at her. The look she gave me said she didn't have any ideas about what the noise was either. I sighed and threw back the covers then rolled out of bed and grabbed my jeans. I pulled them on, tugged a tank top over my head and tossed Rascal her clothes. Once she had them on, we went to investigate, the sounds now joined by slamming cabinets.

I stepped out of my room and saw Angel leaning against the counter in the kitchen, arms folded across her stomach and eyes turned down to the floor. I had opened my mouth to ask her what the hell was going on when I spotted the wet streaks on her cheeks. She had been crying. I moved across the room as Rascal came out of the room behind me and wrapped my best friend in a hug. She put her hands on my shoulders as if she was thinking about pushing me away but then changed her mind and hugged me back. A sob escaped her and she turned her head into my shoulder as she cried.

"Angel, what happened?"

She sobbed for another minute or so and then raised her head to look over my shoulder at Rascal. The slow extended rise and then quick fall of her chest told me she had taken a steadying breath. She gave me a gentle push so I stepped back to give her the space she wanted. Her arms went back to their folded position but she didn't turn her eyes down again, instead looking between Rascal and me. She managed a small smile then reached up to run her fingers through her hair. I didn't push, she would talk when she was ready, she always did.

"I got a call a little while ago."

"I take it the call wasn't good?"

Rascal stepped up beside me as I spoke and slipped her arm around my waist causing the smallest flicker of a smile on Angel's face. It fell away as quickly as it had appeared.

"It was Cassidy."

"Your ex who bailed on you to follow some friends around Europe?"

"Yeah. She's back in town... She wants to see me."

About the Author

Kaden Shay is a 30-something crazy-cat-lady in-the-making who currently resides in Arizona with her partner and miniature zoo, which does currently include 4 cats. When she isn't writing or playing mom to several fur-kids she's singing, playing guitar, or playing online video games.

Kaden grew up in a very musical household and was singing with her family early on in life. Having an English teacher for a dad gave her a love of the written word and encouraged her to begin her own path toward writing. She spent middle school and early high school penning poems, songs, and short stories before beginning her first book at age 16 (a project she still hasn't completed)!

Her furry family, currently consisting of two dogs, four cats, and several rodents, is always available to help her procrastinate in finishing projects.